BOOK

THE FIRST IN A NEW SERIES OF GOTHIC NOVELS BASED ON ABC-TV'S CONTINUING SUSPENSE DRAMA – DARK SHADOWS

Victoria Winters is certain, almost from the very moment of her arrival at sinister Collins House as governess, that she is in terrible danger. Someone in that eerie mansion is determined to see Victoria dead.

But why would anyone want to kill her? Is there something in her past which links her to the strange Collins family? Is she just a chance victim of a ruthless killer? Or has her torment been planned with cruel cunning because she is Victoria Winters?

More frightening still, will she live long enough to find out?

Hermes Press

Originally published 1966

Published by Hermes Press, an imprint of
Herman and Geer Communications, Inc.

Daniel Herman, Publisher
Eileen Sabrina Herman, Managing Editor
Kandice Hartner, Production Manager/Sr. Graphic Designer
Erica McNatt, Copy Editor/Graphic Designer
Jake Merkel, Graphic Designer

2100 Wilmington Road
Neshannock, Pennsylvania 16105
(724) 652-0511
www.HermesPress.com; info@hermespress.com

Book design by Eileen Sabrina Herman
First printing, 2020
Second Printing, 2023

LCCN applied for: 10 9 8 7 6 5 4 3 2 1 0
ISBN 978-1-61345-277-6
OCR and text editing by H + G Media and Eileen Sabrina Herman
Proof reading by Eileen Sabrina Herman and Sara Stein

From Dan, Louise, Sabrina, Jacob, Ruk'us and Noodle for D'zur and Mellow

Acknowledgments: This book would not be possible without the help and encouragement of Jim Pierson and Curtis Holdings

Printed in China

Dark Shadows
by Marilyn Ross

CONTENTS

CHAPTER 1

The ominous clouds of the October afternoon had warned of bad weather on the way and now the threat was being fulfilled. Victoria Winters sat huddled in a corner of the shabby back seat of the taxi that she'd hired in the village to take her to Collins House, aware of the driving rain and high wind that had come with the darkness of early evening. She sat quietly in the shadows, staring at the swaying headlight beams as they cut into the stormy blackness of the uneven road ahead, revealing little but its rutted stony surface and the hostile wet branches of the trees that crowded greedily on either side. Suddenly she was filled with forebodings and began to wonder whether she hadn't made a mistake.

Her decision to accept the position offered as governess at Collins House had been made impulsively. And certainly all that had taken place since she'd embarked on her journey from the New York foundling home where she'd been employed indicated that she might have been too quick in making up her mind. The first clear warning that Collins House might not be all she'd expected had come while she was still on the train from Boston.

A garrulous middle-aged woman who'd introduced herself as Mrs. Mitchell had warned Victoria that Collinsport was a bleak, lonely place much of the year and not even one of the regular train stops.

"Oh, it's pleasant enough in July and August when the tourists come," Mrs. Mitchell had admitted. "But they only stay for nine or ten weeks and then it's dead as a tomb again. A few artists have set up regular homes there, but not many. If it didn't have the Collins Fishing Fleet and the canning plant the place would just fold up. And that's the truth!" Later, when Victoria had left the train at the small wooden shack that served as the Collinsport station, she had stood in the darkness and rain for quite a few minutes before a friendly stranger who had also descended from the train helped her find a taxi. He had seemed startled to find her destination was Collins House, but drove her to the single all-season hotel located on the mean main street of the fishing village. The murky yellow light of its lobby windows and the coffee-shop sign with its single bulb for illumination stood out against the darkness of the rest of the street. Victoria decided that Collinsport must really be an early-to-bed place, since it was no later than nine o'clock at the most.

She had waited in the coffee shop while the stranger went to find the town's only taxi. Sitting on one of the half-dozen stools, she stared at herself in the mirror back of the counter. She was the only customer in the seedy little eating place. Because she was hungry and to fill in the time she had ordered toast and coffee and the pert little waitress was at the end of the counter getting her order ready.

A neon-lighted jukebox gave out with a rock-and-roll tune in the background as Victoria appraised herself in the mirror. It seemed to her that the tiresome train trip and her state of tension had left her looking wan and older than her twenty years. And the rain had done nothing to help her hairdo. The lovely dark hair that tumbled becomingly to her shoulders had a tousled, unkempt look. Her intelligent, somewhat thin face looked disapprovingly at her reflection. She wanted to look her best since in a short time she'd be meeting her new employer, Elizabeth Collins Stoddard.

The mere sound of the name suggested someone stately, cold and demanding. Victoria sighed and her alert green eyes reflected back to her from the mirror with a gleam of dismay in them. She adjusted the belt of her dark blue trench coat and vaguely smoothed the scarf at her throat as she thought of the ordeal ahead.

The waitress returned with the toast and coffee and placed it before her. Pausing to regard her with interest, she asked, "You here visiting someone?"

Victoria took a sip of her coffee and smiled as she reached for a piece of toast. "No. I've come here to take a job."

The waitress looked blank for a moment; then her round face brightened. "Oh! You're going to work at the office down at the canning factory?"

She shook her head. "I'm going to be employed at Collins

House, as a governess for young David Collins. No doubt you've heard of the family."

The waitress registered shock. "You bet I've heard of the family," she said in a surprised voice. With a quick glance around to make sure no one was within listening distance, she added, "You know what you're getting into?"

It was a startling question. Victoria stared at her for a moment. "What do you mean?"

"I mean Collins House is a real kookie place!" the waitress said in the same urgent tone. "It's located on a cliff a couple of miles from town and if ever there was a haunted mansion in this part of Maine, Collins House is it!"

Victoria forced a small smile. "I'm more interested in the people than the house."

"They're oddballs too," the waitress said with a grimace. "Of course, they just about own the town, but people around here don't see much of them. They keep to themselves. And as for that young David you're planning to look after, I've heard he's a regular little monster!"

Victoria's uneasiness grew. "You mean he's deformed in some way?"

"Nothing you'd notice," the waitress said with a wink. "It's inside his head, if you get me. They say he's impossible to manage! As wild as his father and Roger Collins—that's his father—sure has been mixed up in trouble from time to time. He's the only one we see in the village often and then he spends hours on end in the Blue Whale. That's the local bar. Roger sure likes his liquor!"

"What about his wife?"

"They're separated, as far as anyone around here knows," the waitress said. "He used to live in Augusta. He and the boy came here to stay at Collins House a little while back."

"I see," Victoria said slowly. "What about Elizabeth Collins Stoddard?"

The waitress rolled her eyes. "You won't believe this! That woman hasn't left Collins House for eighteen years!"

"Eighteen years!" Victoria gasped, and her thoughts began to race wildly. It all fitted in, matched her own reasons for coming here. "Is she crippled or something?"

"Nothing like that. The story goes that her husband left her one night eighteen years ago and she's never gone out of the house since."

"That's fantastic!"

The waitress shrugged. "Some people think there may be more to it than that. There's been gossip that Elizabeth's husband was murdered. That she may even have had something to do with it and that's why she's acted so strange ever since." Victoria frowned across the counter at the girl. "If there had been anything like that, the police would have found out long ago."

"Don't be too sure. This is isolated country and the Collins family are mighty important people around here. Not many can afford to cross them or question them."

Victoria pushed away her empty coffee cup. "You don't paint a very pleasant picture of Collins House," she said.

The waitress smiled. "Maybe I've made it sound too spooky," she admitted. "After all, there is Carolyn—that's Elizabeth's daughter. She's a swinger and about your age, I'd say."

"That sounds better."

"You'll like Carolyn," the waitress promised. "She's sort of a friend of mine. Tell her you were talking to Maggie Evans."

"I will," Victoria promised. She was about to ask some more questions, but the door from the lobby opened and a tall, lantern-jawed man in a cap and faded blue suit entered.

"You the one waitin' for a taxi, miss?"

Victoria nodded. "Can you take me now?"

"Reckon so," the big man said without enthusiasm. He nodded to the two recently purchased black traveling bags on the floor beside her. "Them your bags?"

"Yes," Victoria said. "You can put them in the car now. I'll be there in a minute."

"Okay, miss," he said in the same sour manner. Picking up a bag in each hand, he went out.

Victoria found the change for her snack and left it on the counter with a tip for Maggie Evans. She smiled at the waitress. "I hope Collins House isn't all you said it is. If I stay, I'll be around to see you later."

"Do that!" Maggie said with a bright smile. "New faces are mighty welcome around here this time of year. And wait until Henry Jones hears where you want him to take you!"

Victoria went out to the taxi and hesitated in the rain long enough to explain where she wanted to be driven. "Collins House," she said. "It's on a side road."

"I know where it is, well enough," the tall man said brusquely with an expression of disdain on his stem face. "I can't imagine anyone wanting to go there on a night like this!" He was still grumbling to himself as he opened the door for her to get into the taxi.

It had only been a few minutes until they turned off the main street and began the difficult journey along the narrow, gravel road. Then, seated in the almost complete darkness of the cab, she had leaned back with closed eyes and reviewed the events that had brought her here to this remote fishing village on the Maine coast.

The letter had been addressed to her at the foundling home where she had been raised and where she had returned to teach after taking training. In a sense it was the only home she had ever known and Charles Fairweather, the elderly lawyer who directed the affairs of the home, had always been like a father to her. She had at once gone to his office and shown him the letter from Collinsport written on a fine vellum in Elizabeth Stoddard's neat handwriting.

Charles Fairweather had donned his horn-rimmed glasses and scanned the letter quickly. Then he'd glanced up at her with a smile on his lined, friendly face. "It sounds like a most interesting offer," he said. "And the salary mentioned is better than we are paying you here. Do you plan to accept?"

Victoria's sensitive features had shown her inner struggle as she said, "I'm thinking of it. But not because it offers more money. My reason would be that Collinsport is only fifty miles from Bangor."

The old man's eyebrows raised. "Fifty miles from Bangor," he repeated. And then, as if something had suddenly dawned on him, he said quickly, "Of course!"

"It may have something to do with the money that was sent from there each month."

"I wouldn't jump to that conclusion," the old lawyer warned.

"But there must be some reason why this woman should write me," Victoria said. "I mean, why should she single me out for the position? How would she know about me?"

Charles Fairweather glanced at the letter again. "It says here that you were suggested to her by a friend of the home," he said. "I'd consider that explanation enough. We have a large board of directors and patrons in every section of the country. Many of them visit here and I may say I frequently comment on your excellent teaching ability."

Victoria smiled. "You're too generous. And you may be right. But I have the strange feeling this may have something to do with my past, that this may be a link that will clear up the mystery of who I really am."

The old man looked sad. "I suppose that does bother you," he agreed, "although I believe you are wrong to let it make you unhappy. Why not be content that you are Victoria Winters, a lovely young woman with above-average abilities and a fine future ahead? Why grieve about a past that may always remain shrouded in mystery?"

Victoria sighed. "I wish I could feel that way. It would be a lot easier. But there are times when I wonder, when I feel incomplete. I don't care what the truth about my parents might be. I'd just like to know and have it settled."

The old man folded his hands and nodded. "I know how it is. I've heard the same story from too many of our charges. But I must warn you"—he looked up at her with solemn eyes —"that the few who have learned the truth about themselves have not always been made happier by it."

"I realize that," she admitted. "And yet the feeling is still there. I want to find out who I am and why I was left here. It isn't enough to know I was left here twenty years ago in a basket with the message, 'Her name is Victoria Winters. I can't take care of her.' My mother and father may still be alive. I'd like to find them and learn why I was deserted."

Charles Fairweather tapped the letter. "I wouldn't base any hopes on this."

"Perhaps not," she said. "But it is near Bangor. I could ask questions and make some visits there. Who knows what I may discover?"

He spread his hands in a gesture of resignation. "Who knows, indeed? It is a fact that for fourteen years twenty dollars a month was mailed to you here in a plain envelope with a typed address and a Bangor postmark. So someone in Bangor knew you and also knew that you were here. But it doesn't have to mean that the money was sent to you by one or the other of your parents."

"I think you'll agree it was someone with a serious concern for my welfare," Victoria said. "And I believe this will be my chance to find out who it was. So I think I'll take the job Mrs. Stoddard is offering me."

He handed her the letter. "If that is your decision," he said heavily. "Keep in touch with me and let us help you, if the job doesn't turn out. You can always come back."

Victoria smiled her gratitude. Charles Fairweather was a fine old man whose first concern had always been for his charges. He devoted far more of his energy to his position as head of the foundling home than was required of him, and he did so with obvious enjoyment.

She said, "Thank you. You can be sure you'll hear from me, however it turns out."

The cab hit an unusually bad bump in the road and jolted her back to the present, a present that was more than a little frightening. She glanced out into the rainy darkness and wondered just what it would be like at Collins House. Had she been foolhardy in accepting the job? Would it wind up with her placing herself in physical danger and finding out nothing about her past?

She refused to believe this. As the days had passed, she had become more convinced that the secret of her identity might at last be revealed to her at Collins House. In her more romantic and imaginative moments she pictured herself as the long-lost daughter of Elizabeth Collins Stoddard. Now, as she neared her destination and had learned of Elizabeth's daughter, Caroline, this hope had ebbed considerably. But she still felt there must be some link with the past in the old house, that the vital clue to her identity would be found there.

The cabby, Henry Jones, was hunched over the wheel. Now he turned his head slightly and spoke above the noise of the engine. "You some relation to the Collins clan?"

Victoria smiled ruefully in the darkness. "No," she said.

"Hope you got some good reason for visiting them," he said. "If you expect to sell them anything, you're just plain out of luck. They don't let any sales people or anyone else into the place. You might just as well turn around and go back to the hotel."

"I'm expected. I'm the new governess for David Collins."

Jones shook his head, keeping his eyes fastened on the road. "That brat!" he said. "You'll have your hands full. The Collins family ain't what they used to be."

"Why do you say that?"

He snorted. "Because it's the truth! Like all the old-line families around here, they've just naturally gone to seed. I'll bet if old Jeremiah Collins was alive he'd have a stroke. He's the one who built the place way back in 1830."

"It's a very old house then," she said.

"Lots older in Maine," he said laconically. "Some places date back to 1700 and around then. But there ain't many of them big as Collins House. It's got forty rooms, although I doubt if they use half of them now."

"Forty rooms!"

"And one servant!" the cab driver chuckled. "Figure that one out! Not that they couldn't afford plenty if they wanted them. But old Elizabeth is peculiar. You've heard about her not leaving the place for eighteen years, I guess."

"Just recently," Victoria said in an awed voice. "So it's true?"

"You bet," the driver said grimly. "She ain't set a foot out of that spooky place since her hubby vanished one night. And the next day she dismissed all the servants. Now they only got Matt Morgan to do the rough chores and he ain't more than three-quarters bright. Used to work with him when we were both at the cannery. One of them surly types."

Victoria heard the cab driver's comments with growing alarm. It struck her that the people at Collins House must be as strange as the old mansion itself. But perhaps this was only because they preferred to keep themselves apart from the village. Small town people would not understand this attitude and so build a mystery where none existed.

"We'll soon be within sight of Widow's Hill," Henry Jones said as he drove on.

"Widow's Hill?"

"The cliff where Collins House stands," he said. "Been a lot of strange things happened there over the years. First, Josette, the wife of Jeremiah Collins, who built the place, threw herself off the cliff on a stormy night. Maybe one a lot like this."

Victoria shivered. "Why?"

"Not properly certain," Henry Jones said. "Such a long time back. But I reckon from what the old folks said she was lonely and frightened. Jeremiah was smart in business but a cold man. And she was French and strange to these shores. It ended with her throwing herself down that hundred-foot cliff into the ocean." He paused. "She wasn't the only one. There've been a couple of other strange deaths on the cliff. The last one was only last year and a Collins was mixed up in it."

"Who?" Victoria asked with growing fear.

But she was given no reply, for at that very moment there was a pounding from the rear wheel on her side, a pounding so regular it could not be explained by the rough surface of the road. A tire had surely gone flat. Henry Jones gave vent to an angry groan and brought the car to a halt.

"Flat tire, sure as shootin'," he said gloomily as he hesitated behind the wheel a minute. "And this sure is some night to have to change it."

With the motor stopped, the sound of the rain came even more plainly. She felt sorry for Jones. "Let me hold the flashlight for you," she suggested.

"If I can find one," he said gloomily, reaching for the glove compartment at the same time. A few minutes later she was standing in the cold rain with the flashlight directed on the wheel as he went grumpily about the task of jacking up the car. She hugged her trench coat about her and stared into the surrounding darkness as he worked on.

At last he turned to her in disgust. "I can't move these studs," he said. "They put them on with an electric wrench and my wheel wrench won't touch them. I guess we're stuck for certain."

"But there must be some way!" she protested.

"There are three ways," he advised her bitterly. "We can sit here on our sterns until morning and I can go for help; we can walk the rest of the mile and a half to Collins House, or we can try driving there on the rim, if you want to buy me a new wheel."

"Perhaps we'd better walk then," she said.

He looked grim as small rivulets of rain streaked down his weathered cheeks. "It's a long haul in this weather and the wind will be a lot stronger and nastier as you get closer to the cliff."

Victoria glanced despairingly at the wheel. "You're sure you can't move those bolts?"

"Never was more certain of anything," he said. Then his attention seemed to be suddenly caught by something ahead on the road. He jabbed a finger into the darkness excitedly. "Looks like we're in luck," he exclaimed. "There's a car coming this way from the house."

Victoria peered into the night. "I don't see any sign of it."

"Watch!" he advised her. "Now! See!" As he spoke she did see the gleam of headlights in the sky. A moment later they came into full view. Henry Jones hastened to turn on his own headlights and then, taking the flashlight from her, ran ahead to wave the oncoming car down.

It came to a stop about twenty feet from them and Victoria watched as a tall, slim man got out quickly and approached Henry Jones. He spoke in a pleasant, rather deep voice. "What's the trouble, Henry?"

"Flat! And my tire wrench ain't any good," the cab driver said plaintively.

The tall man nodded. "I'll get mine. It's a four-way. Should do the trick."

The two men went to work at the wheel as Victoria stood in the background and again held the flashlight. She caught a glimpse of the tall man and saw that he had a good-natured, rather boyish face, but he handled himself with an air of authority. He was well dressed, obviously not a fisherman type, and since his sleek gray car had been coming from the direction of Collins House she found herself wondering if he mightn't be a member of the family.

This question was answered for her in the next moment. Having changed the tire, the young man stood up and turned to her. "I'm Will Grant," he told her. "I suppose you're the new governess. Miss Winters. Elizabeth was worrying about you when I left."

"That's right," she smiled. "I am Victoria Winters. I was slow getting a taxi and then we had this accident."

Will Grant laughed in a low, pleasant fashion. "Elizabeth will understand," he assured her. "She was only concerned about your welfare. You should have no more trouble now. I'm a lawyer for a few of the Collins interests, by the way." Henry Jones had put the flat tire and tools in the trunk and now came around to join them and say, "Sure obliged to you, Will. Reckon we'd have been here all night if you hadn't come along."

"Glad to have been able to help," he said. With a glance Victoria's way he added, "We'll be seeing each other again. Miss Winters. I have to visit the house a good deal and it will be nice to have a new face on hand during this dreary season." He hesitated, a twinkle in his eyes. "Especially a face as lovely as yours!" With that he nodded and started back to his own car, leaving Victoria staring after him in some confusion.

At her side Henry Jones grunted. "Will has a way with the women!" he told her. "I guess we better get in the car and get it moved out of the way." Victoria quickly obeyed him and returned to the rear seat. A moment later the big gray car went by them and Will Grant honked the horn lightly and waved to her in passing.

"He seems very nice," Victoria observed as the cab resumed its journey again.

"Will is all right," Henry Jones said. "Reckon he can nab young Carolyn for a wife if he's willing to wait a couple of years until she's a little older. Her mother likes Will and she'd probably agree to the match."

Victoria was not entirely pleased at the tone in which the cab driver had made the remark. She had the feeling that Will Grant's behavior was being misconstrued.

She asked mildly, "How do you think he feels about the idea?"

"I guess maybe he isn't much interested," Henry Jones admitted. "He's on the go a lot. Always off to Boston and New York on company business."

"I see," Victoria said, secretly pleased at forcing him to acquit the young man of the charge that he might be a fortune-hunter. Will Grant had not impressed her as being that type at all. She went on, "If he's a sample of the people at Collins House, they can't be so awful!"

"He's not a Collins," the driver snorted. "Though some of them seem pleasant enough at first meeting. Take Ernest Collins, the one that's a concert violinist. He's got his place closed up now and is living with the others at the big house. Ernest was a nice boy and I still like him. But he's been peculiar ever since he lost his wife in that car accident in California. Came back here and shut up his own big house and only turns up here between concert seasons these days."

"You say he is at the house now?" she asked.

He nodded. "Yep. As I said, I like Ernest, or I did until that summer girl went over the cliff last year. Artist she was, and pretty, too. She and Ernest were always together. She had rented one of the stone cottages on the place, the mate to Matt Morgan's, and she painted some pretty pictures. Then one foggy night she went over the cliff. They found her body on the rocks at low tide. The police questioned Ernest, but they weren't able to connect him with it. Elizabeth claimed she saw the girl go for a walk alone after Ernest had gone to bed." He paused. "But a lot of people around here think Ernest hasn't been right in the head since his wife was killed and they got ideas of what might have happened to that girl."

A cold tremor passed through her. "It's an ugly story," she said.

"You'll hear more of them if you stay at Collins House," the cab driver warned her as they rounded a comer of the narrow road. "There it is. Up on the hill!"

The trees lining the road gave way to open fields at this point and as Victoria peered ahead she was able, even in the darkness, to distinguish the great, square hulk of Collins House, looming on the crest of the rocky cliff known as Widow's Hill. Its tall chimneys streaked up to mingle with the utter blackness of the sky and the faint outline of the captain's walk on its main building was barely discernible. The place was as huge and majestic as she'd been told it would be and was built in the style of an English manor house.

As they drove nearer they took a curving carriage road that led directly to the front entrance. A gust of rain struck the windows of the car and the wind whistled like a banshee. It was a lonely and isolated spot. Only one window on the lower floor showed a light; except for that, the great mansion was in complete darkness.

"They don't keep the grounds up like they used to," Henry Jones told her. "And I hear a lot of the house is shut off. The gardens are overgrown with weeds. They need a staff to keep up the place and all they have is Matt Morgan."

He brought the cab to a halt before the front door and quickly got out and opened the rear car door for Victoria. She stood still for a moment, studying the great building with a new feeling of uneasiness. There was something eerie about the old house. She hesitated, noting the dimly lighted window to the right of the main entrance and the total absence of any light near the door itself. As she stood there Henry Jones was already taking the bags from the cab. He put them down beside her and she paid him.

He took the money, and glancing toward the building, said, "You sure they're expecting you?"

"Of course," she said, turning to him in the semi-darkness. "You heard Mr. Grant say they were."

The weathered, lined face of the cab driver showed a strange expression of dread. "In that case, there isn't any use of me waiting," he said. Before she could offer any objection," he tipped his cap and hurriedly went off and got behind the wheel again.

She watched with dismay as he started the car and the red taillights began to fade in the distance. Gathering her courage, she

quickly advanced up the front steps and rang the bell. Far off inside
the house she could hear the weak sound of its ring. She waited in
the darkness, growing more tense with each passing moment. Then
she rang the bell again. Glancing behind her nervously, she saw
that the taxi was no longer in sight. Henry Jones had not wanted
to linger on the grounds. Still no one had come in answer to her
summons. She was about to try the bell again when she noticed a
light in a side door of the wing to the right. The door was at lawn
level and it seemed someone was standing in the entrance, holding
a flashlight or lantern. But she decided to go to it at once, thinking
Mrs. Stoddard might have decided to meet her at this side entrance.
Victoria hurried down the stairs and started across the lawn in the
direction of the other entrance. But as she did so, the light that had
drawn her attention vanished abruptly. She gave a small gasp that
was somewhere between fear and annoyance and hurried on in the
darkness. Then, without warning, she was roughly grasped from
behind and held by cruelly strong hands that dug into her flesh.
Stricken with terror, she cried out.

CHAPTER 2

Victoria struggled vainly to free herself from the hands that held her in their fierce grip. Visions of all the horror enveloping the sinister old house passed through her mind in rapid succession. She had been warned of the unknown danger awaiting her and yet she had chosen to walk blindly into it. With another frantic cry of terror she made a fresh effort to escape.

"No need for alarm," a male voice told her urgently. "I'm trying to help you, not hurt you!" At the same time she was dragged back a foot or two and the hands eased their grip on her.

Something in the cultured voice at once eased her fears. Still shaken, she glanced around to see a thin, shadowy figure outlined behind her.

The man spoke again and this time apologetically. "I must ask your pardon for coming up behind you and grasping you the way I did. But I had no choice. You were on the edge of danger."

Staring at him, Victoria finally asked in a small voice, "What are you talking about?"

The man waved to the spot where she'd been standing before. "You were walking directly toward an old well whose wooden covering has rotted away to the point where I doubt if it would stand even your light weight. It was too late to do anything but grab you and haul you back." He paused. "I'm sorry I wasn't a little more gentle about it."

Victoria felt embarrassed as she realized the truth of the situation. It had really been her own fault for leaving the front steps and hurrying across in the darkness toward the will-of-the-wisp light that had so quickly vanished. She had thoughtlessly made a move that could have cost her her life, had it not been for the prompt action of this stranger.

"I didn't mean to make such a fuss," she said weakly. "And thank you for what you did."

"I'm only glad I was here to do it," he said. "There have been enough accidents here without another being added.

I imagine you are the governess my cousin has been expecting. I am Ernest Collins."

Victoria couldn't help asking, "The violinist?"

"The same," he said, sounding rather pleased. "Don't tell me you've heard of me."

She thought it prudent to let him think the only knowledge she had of him was of his professional life. She said, "After all, you are fairly well known."

"I suppose so," he said doubtfully. "At least in music circles." He took her by the arm, lightly this time. "I'm sure Elizabeth must have heard your screams and be at the front door by now."

Victoria let him lead her toward the main entrance again, feeling more ashamed of her hysterical performance than before. When they reached the bottom of the steps she saw that the large oak door had been opened and the stately silhouette of a female figure stood outlined against the dim foyer light. Victoria's heart began to beat a little more rapidly at the sight of Elizabeth Stoddard.

Ernest Collins let her arm go and said quietly, "I'll follow with your bags, Miss Winters."

In a sort of daze Victoria slowly mounted the several steps until she was face to face with the slim older woman. Then she said haltingly, "I'm Victoria Winters."

"I'm glad you are finally here, Miss Winters," the woman said in a cool, controlled voice. "I'm Elizabeth Stoddard. Won't you come in."

Victoria moved slowly forward and Ernest Collins followed with her bags, which he put at the base of the stairway directly ahead. She turned to Elizabeth and said, "I'm sorry I raised such a fuss. I almost walked into an old well and Mr. Collins came to my rescue. I misinterpreted his action and cried out." "It is a foul night and I could hardly have expected that sort of danger," Elizabeth said, as she carefully closed and bolted the main door. Turning to Victoria again, she asked, "But what were you doing in that area of the lawn?"

Glancing toward Ernest Collins, who now stood regarding

them with quiet interest, she told Elizabeth, "I waited and no one answered the bell. Then I saw a light at a side door." Elizabeth frowned. She had plainly been a beauty in her young days and even now was a strikingly lovely woman with a proud, upright bearing and an aura of the aristocrat about her. This was no ordinary woman. She exuded strength, power and determination. Victoria judged she would be in her mid-fifties, yet there were only slight lines of pain around her mouth to mar her beauty and betray her age.

Elizabeth said, "I'm sorry I was so long answering the door. I heard the bell but I was detained upstairs. But you must be wrong about having seen a light in that side entrance. That wing is shut off. Has been for some time. No one could have been there."

"But I'm certain," Victoria protested weakly.

Ernest Collins came to her rescue with a slight smile on his handsome, sensitive face. He told his cousin, "You can see that I've badly frightened Miss Winters and I don't think she should be questioned too much about details at this point. No doubt she saw the headlights of the cab as it turned, reflected in the glass of the side entrance door. This place is spooky enough at any time. No wonder she was terrified on such a night. Let her get some rest and she'll feel better when she sees the place in morning sunshine."

Elizabeth listened to him with a thoughtful expression; then she smiled faintly. "Of course Ernest is right. But then, he usually is. I take it you two have introduced yourselves."

He laughed easily. "Under the most startling conditions." Victoria managed a small smile of her own. "A lucky meeting for me." She was going to add that she was certain about having seen the ghostly light, but decided it would be unwise. She knew it hadn't been the reflection of the lights of the turning cab. The cab had already been gone several minutes before she'd noticed the blue glow. But she sensed that Ernest had come to her rescue at a difficult moment and it would be best to let things remain as they were.

The older woman gave her cousin a searching glance. "What were you doing prowling around in the rain and darkness, Ernest?"

His serious face showed a hint of being caught off guard. He spoke up too quickly. "I had another of my headaches. I needed some fresh air."

Elizabeth regarded him with mild surprise. "At least you should have put on a raincoat," she told him.

He shrugged. "You know how I am sometimes." Turning to Victoria, he added, "If you'll excuse me, Miss Winters, I'll go upstairs and change. My clothes are drenched through." He glanced Elizabeth's way. "If you'll tell me where Miss Winters' room is. I'll take up her bags and put them in it."

"On the second floor," the slim woman said. "The first door on the left and directly opposite David's." It was the first mention she had made of the boy whom Victoria had come to look after.

Ernest picked up the bags again. "Fine," he said. "I'll leave them there." And he started upstairs.

There was a long moment of silence between the two women until he had gone out of sight. All this time Victoria was aware that the older woman was studying her appraisingly. And for the first time she was able to take in the richness of her surroundings. The foyer walls were done in walnut paneling, which served as a background for a series of paintings of fishing ships and portraits of long-dead members of the Collins family. A magnificent crystal chandelier hung overhead, but its impressiveness was spoiled by the fact that it was not fully lighted and gave off only a dull glow.

"You must forgive my cousin," Elizabeth said at last, glancing cautiously toward the stairs to make certain he was no longer close enough to overhear them. "He is weary from a long concert tour. Too, he has known a great deal of personal sorrow in the past few years and it has left him tense, quite unlike his normal self."

"That is too bad," Victoria said politely, not sure what the mistress of Collins House was trying to convey. Turning to the giant grandfather's clock that stood near the bottom of the stairs, she exclaimed, "What a fine old clock! They always interest me!"

Elizabeth continued to study her in her cool way. "We have many valuable items in the house," she said, "Some of them in the wing that is closed off."

"It's such a large place," Victoria said. "Is it forty rooms you have?"

"Yes. With one male servant, you can understand why most of them are not in use. You must be cold. I've some tea ready. Please go into the drawing room I'll be with you in a moment."

She went off down the narrow hall that evidently led to the rear of the house.

Victoria watched her go, still somewhat dazed by the excitement of her entrance into the old mansion. Ernest Collins had been very nice and seemed anxious to be helpful to her. Why had Elizabeth made that odd apology for him? He was tense, she had said, and a little strange. Unbidden into her head came the thought of what the cab driver had suggested— that he was locally suspected of murder. She brushed the thought aside angrily. After the way he had rescued her, it was most uncharitable to remember such gossip.

She slowly entered the drawing room and was again confronted by richly paneled walls and portraits of Collins' forebears staring grimly down at her from gold frames. For no apparent reason a small shiver went through her. She wondered if the blood of these long-dead ancestors of the Collins family might also course in her own veins. Was she a lost member of the family? Had her hope of finding the truth here been a vain one? Would she ever know?

She was standing with her back to the doorway and suddenly heard a footstep behind her. She turned quickly to discover Elizabeth standing there with a tea tray. The older woman came into the room and set the tray down on a table. She nodded to the portrait of a severe-faced, gray-mustached man on the wall opposite.

"That's the man who built Collins House," she said. "My great-grandfather, Jeremiah Collins. He was one of the most outstanding of our line. It was he who began the fishing firm, as well. My own father developed the canning end of it into a world-wide business." She filled two of the cups and asked, "Do you prefer your tea with lemon or cream?"

"Lemon, please."

Elizabeth handed her the cup and they sat down facing each other. The older woman said, "I hoped my brother, Roger, would be here to meet you. It is his boy, David, who will be in your care. But he seems to have wandered off somewhere." Victoria took a sip of her tea. "There'll be plenty of time," she said. "How old is David?"

"He is nine," Mrs. Stoddard said with another slight frown. "I am a frank woman, Miss Winters. And I intend to be frank now. You will find the boy difficult. Extremely difficult."

"Most boys are at his age," she suggested with a smile.

"David is no ordinary boy," the other woman said. "He is clever enough. Perhaps too clever for his age. But he has an unhappy, resentful quality about him that is most unpleasant. I have warned his father if you are unable to manage him, he must be sent to boarding school. Indeed, that is where I feel he should be now."

"What are his father's views?"

"Roger has no particular interest in the boy," Elizabeth said, staring down at the steaming cup of tea. "Since he and his wife separated, my brother seems to have actually taken a dislike to David."

Victoria thought it strange the boy was not with his mother but felt it would be wise to postpone any questions on this subject until later. She had the idea Elizabeth had purposely been vague in referring to Roger's absent wife and would not relish being questioned about her further. It was sufficient that the unhappy little boy was here in the house and about to come under her care. The other things that might have a bearing on the problem of David could be discovered later. Perhaps she might learn a good deal from the boy.

Victoria's thoughts were interrupted by the sounds of measured, heavy steps coming down the stairs. She turned to Elizabeth with a questioning glance. The older woman already had her eyes fixed on the doorway and was showing a degree of nervousness.

Then a new figure appeared in the doorway. Victoria guessed it was the missing Roger Collins, younger brother to Elizabeth and father of David. He was fair-haired and probably close to forty, with Elizabeth's even good looks, but with a trace of weakness in his face that Victoria had not found in that of the mistress of Collins House. His cheeks were flushed now and his eyes seemed to pop a trifle as he stood swaying in the doorway with a drunken, silly smile.

"I've been wondering where you were, Roger," Elizabeth said with a hint of annoyance. "This is Miss Victoria Winters, the new governess. My brother, Roger."

Roger came forward carefully managing not to stagger, but only by a hair. "Delighted to meet you, Miss Winters," he said, offering his hand. "Would you care for a brandy?"

"Thank you. I'm enjoying my tea," she told him.

The blond man nodded agreeably. "Well, then. I'll just treat myself to one," he said. And at once moved across the room to the mahogany sideboard on which a group of several cut-glass decanters and glasses were set out.

As he poured himself a drink his sister said sharply, "It seems to me you've been treating yourself too generously already."

Roger held the glass between his hands and bent his head to enjoy the bouquet. "Do not nag me, sister dear," he said. "I drink merely to forget and in this house one must do a lot of drinking— there is so much to forget." He gulped down most of the brandy and then stared owlishly at Victoria. "You're very young," he said. "I doubt if you'll do. In fact, I have been opposed to your coming at all. We have enough problems here without–"

"Roger!" his sister said sharply, interrupting him before he could finish. "We have heard quite enough from you on that subject."

He gestured weakly. "As you say, Elizabeth. I will not bother to tell Miss Winters that my son is a little monster who hates his father and just about everything else. I will not warn her that she would be wise to give up the job before she begins and leave this house."

Victoria frowned in astonishment. "But I thought you really wanted me. The letter I received at the foundling home said that someone had suggested me as the right person for your son."

"That is true," Elizabeth said quickly. "Someone did."

"Who?" Victoria asked at once, feeling she might be on the verge of an important disclosure.

The older woman's tragic, beautiful face took on a shadow. "I don't know exactly," she said with the vagueness she'd affected before and which did not fit in with her personality. "I forget."

"It's important to me that I know," Victoria insisted.

Elizabeth eyed her suspiciously. "Why should it be important?"

Impulsively Victoria decided to tell them. She gave a brief recital of her past and the mystery of the monthly payment of twenty dollars that had come to her from nearby Bangor. She explained how desperately anxious she was to find out who she really was, learn her true identity.

Elizabeth had listened to her account with no betraying expression, her hands folded in her lap. Roger had filled in the time by helping himself to another brandy.

When she finished he regarded her bleakly and said, "Fantastic! Sounds like the first act of 'East Lynne' or some other Victorian melodrama. You mean to say you were actually a foundling?"

"She has already said it," Elizabeth snapped. Turning to Victoria, she added, "I can understand your concern and I appreciate your desire to discover more about yourself, but I don't think you should build any hopes on the mere fact this village happens to be only a short distance from Bangor."

Victoria's disappointment showed in her face. "I've been counting on it," she said.

"I hope that wasn't your only reason for accepting my offer," Elizabeth said.

"It wasn't," she protested. "But I won't deny it helped me decide to come."

"My advice to you is the same as that of the Mr. Fairweather whom you mentioned," the older woman said. "I would concentrate on the future and not worry about the past."

"Few of us can do that," Roger mumbled over his glass.

His sister darted him a crushing look. There was something in Elizabeth's reaction to her story that made Victoria feel the older woman had not been frank with her this time. She was convinced that Elizabeth might know something about her origin that she was not revealing. If she waited long enough and was patient enough, she might discover what it was.

Elizabeth said, "You have still to meet my daughter, Carolyn. She's in the village for the evening, having a date with Joe Haskell, a local boy. You'll like her, I know. She's only a little younger than you and she's been looking forward to your coming."

Roger had put down his glass and was now staring intently at a portrait which was from an early period, but which bore a startling likeness to him. He swung around to Victoria and said, "See him? That's old Isaac Collins! First of the line! Landed here before the Mayflower dropped anchor and founded Collinsport. We'd all have been better off if the Indians had scalped him and ended the whole business before it began."

"I assume you're speaking for yourself, Roger," his sister said acidly as she got up. "I'll take you to your room now, Miss Winters."

"Thank you," she said and rising followed the older woman out.

"Bolt your door well, Miss Winters," Roger called after her drunkenly. "It'll make you feel better, anyway, even if it doesn't lock out the ghosts!"

Nothing was said between the two women until they were on the stairs. Then Elizabeth said primly, "You mustn't pay any attention to Roger. Especially ignore anything he may have said tonight. When he is drinking he is not himself at all. You'll find him a completely different person in the morning."

"I understand," Victoria said quietly. Privately she was thinking that Roger would only make a difficult household more difficult. There was no question that he was a problem drinker and she could expect him to be "not himself" more often than not.

Elizabeth led her up the dimly lighted stairway and they took a sharp turn left to a corridor with doors opening off each side of it. Elizabeth went directly to the first door on the left and opened it.

"This will be your room," she said. "And I see Ernest was as good as his word. Your bags are already in here."

Victoria quickly took in the fair-sized room, furnished plainly with antiques. There was a four-poster bed, a tall chest of drawers, an easy chair for reading, a Tiffany-style lamp on a small table beside it, casement windows that opened into the room. One of them had been blown open by the wind; rain had come in and the room was damp and chilled.

Elizabeth went quickly to the window and shut it. "I must speak to Matt about the catch on this window," she said. "He promised to fix it before you arrived, but you can't always depend on him. I hope you like the room?"

"It's luxurious by my standards," Victoria assured her. "Our rooms at the home are pretty Spartan."

A touch of sympathy showed on the older woman's lovely face. "I suppose so," she said. Glancing around, she added, "I picked this for you because it is a room that has always had a special meaning for me. When I was growing up, this was my room."

"I'm glad you chose it for me," Victoria said, struck by Elizabeth's attitude. It contained some of the solicitude you might expect in a mother—mother still holding back her carefully controlled love, but betraying herself in small ways. She wondered if it could be.

"The nights sometimes get cold at this season." Elizabeth quickly walked over to the closet and opened its door. "You'll find extra blankets in here if you need them."

"I'm sure I'll be very comfortable."

Elizabeth gave her one of her familiar searching looks. Very quietly she said, "I hope so."

Victoria said, "I think you mentioned David's room is directly across from this one. That should make it convenient."

"True." Elizabeth started for the door, then hesitated when she'd almost reached it and turned to Victoria again. "I must warn you not to try to rush things with the boy. Let him get used to you first."

"I'll remember."

"He's not really a bad child," Elizabeth went on with a touch of agitation, quite foreign to her, showing in her manner. "His life hasn't been too happy so far. I'd like to see it improve here."

"No doubt the previous governess left a record of how he'd progressed with his studies," Victoria suggested. "It would be helpful to have any such information."

Elizabeth nodded. "His lesson books and her notes are in the study downstairs." She paused. "Miss Gordon left rather unexpectedly. A misunderstanding with my brother."

"Oh!" Victoria said politely. She didn't need to probe into the matter any further. Her short meeting with Roger Collins had shown her what a difficult person he was.

"But things should be much better, now that you're here," Elizabeth said with a brighter expression. "Somehow you seem very right for the position and for this house."

Again Victoria was taken by the way in which the older woman spoke, and again she wondered. She said, "I have a good deal of experience with all types of youngsters. I'm certain David and I will get along well."

"We'll have you two meet in the morning," Elizabeth said. "But I'd prefer your taking a few days to know each other before you begin a regular routine of studies." She paused. "Don't allow yourself to be overwhelmed by the fact we may seem a rather strange lot. And don't be frightened of this forbidding old house."

The words came so unexpectedly that it took Victoria a moment to adjust. With a hesitant smile she said, "Thank you. I'm sure I'll feel very much at home here."

Elizabeth became her stern self again. "I wouldn't be quite that optimistic," she said grimly. "But don't let your imagination get the better of you, as it did earlier this evening. In spite of the gossip in Collinsport, we are not all insane nor does the house abound with ghosts. So if a window blows open or you hear a soft footstep or a creaking floorboard, accept them for what they are and you'll find yourself much happier here." It was difficult for Victoria to find an answer to this extraordinary declaration. She settled for a quiet, "Thank you."

The older woman opened the door. "Goodnight, then." With her hand still on the knob, she added, "Of course, you should follow

Roger's advice and bolt your door. Not for the reason he gave, but because young David is an early riser and a prowler. He might decide to snoop in here."

She smiled. "Thank you for the warning."

"He has also been known to take things from rooms," Elizabeth went on. "Not necessarily things of value, but just for the prank of it. Miss Gordon had a bad time when he stole a valued cameo left by her grandmother. Of course he returned it after the poor girl had been reduced to tears. I'd keep any important personal items locked in one of your suitcases."

"I will," Victoria said, shocked by Elizabeth's calm revelations about the youngster. It seemed David might be even more of a problem than she'd expected.

"There's a washbasin in the corner and the bathroom is the third door down on this side of the hall, just past Carolyn's room," Elizabeth said. With a final "Goodnight" she went out, closing the door after her.

Victoria stood staring at the closed door for a full moment after the mistress of Collins House had gone. The old mansion was quite different from what she'd expected and yet it obviously cloaked plenty of secrets. She had learned enough in the short time since she'd arrived to convince her of that.

Elizabeth Stoddard had struck her as being an especially unhappy person, whose strength of character had enabled her to stand up to troubles that would have probably crushed the average individual. Her emotions had been kept in check so long she now presented an almost icy exterior. Yet there were moments when her feelings seeped through. And Victoria could not help feeling drawn toward the attractive older woman. More than ever she was convinced Elizabeth might hold the key to her past. It seemed almost certain that her being summoned to Collins House was no mere chance happening.

The hints given her about the boy to be in her charge were not heartening. David Collins sounded almost as difficult as his father. But perhaps Elizabeth was right, perhaps the boy would react to affection and come around.

She would be fair and reserve final judgment on Roger Collins until she had met and talked with him when he was sober. But his actions downstairs and the hasty reference Elizabeth had made to his difficulty with the previous governess could only be regarded as warnings.

So far the person who had made the most favorable impression on her at Collins House was Ernest Collins, the cousin. The young concert violinist had seemed a pleasant and considerate person and he had surely prevented her from having a bad accident;

had, perhaps, saved her life. He was as handsome in a dark, sensitive way as the cab driver had described him. She had particularly noticed the long, slender, white fingers that no doubt served him in good stead as a musician and yet had such strength in them.

But even Ernest Collins could not be thought of as a completely normal person. The cab driver had been emphatic in mentioning the change in him since the tragic death of his lovely wife. Certainly this was shown in the fact that he'd closed his own house and come to live with the other branch of his family. And his wandering about in the rain without a hat or coat was surely strange. In the back of her mind was also the dark remembrance of the romance he'd had with the attractive girl artist last summer and the suspicious circumstances of her death. She frowned. She refused to think of Ernest as a possible murderer.

Crossing the softly lighted room, she drew back one of the curtains from the casement window and stared out into the night. The rain seemed to have ended, but there was still a high wind that whistled eerily about the old mansion. Straining her eyes, she was able to make out the edge of the cliff and the ocean beyond. Even though the grounds were said to have been allowed to run down, she would still enjoy a tour of them and the view of the sea in daylight.

All at once she realized how weary she was and with a deep sigh let the curtain fall back in place. She went over to her bags and for the next half-hour busied herself with unpacking. She was careful to allow a leather box with some important personal items to remain in one of her suitcases, which she locked and placed in the rear of the closet. When she'd finished settling in, she changed to her dressing gown and left the room to make her way to the bathroom. She'd only started down the corridor when she heard a creaking of a door behind her. Turning quickly, she saw that the door to young David's room had opened an inch or two. She stared at it for a moment and then decided to ignore the fact that the boy was spying on her.

When she returned from the bathroom she paused at her own door. The door opposite was closed tightly again. A look of weary resignation crossed her pretty face. While she didn't like the idea of being spied on, she supposed she couldn't blame the youngster for being curious.

Within a few moments she was in bed with the light turned off. Not until she stared up at the blackness of the room from her pillow did she become uneasy. Only then did she realize how vulnerable she was in this mansion of mystery. But she recalled Elizabeth's calm words of caution and fought back her fears. Her fatigue brought the curtain down on her troubled thoughts as her eyelids closed and she dropped into a deep sleep.

CHAPTER 3

She was not sure what woke her up so suddenly. Her frightened eyes searched the darkness as she drew the bed coverings protectively to her. At first all she heard was the wind and the banging of a distant shutter. Deciding this was what had awakened her, she sank back on her pillow. And then a quite different sound came to her from across the room. It was a scraping sound, like the scraping of long finger nails against polished wood. It went on frantically for seconds and then to her utter horror was followed by what seemed shuffling footsteps, coming closer to her. She choked with fear. Most terrifying of all, she felt the bed vibrate, as if an unsteady hand had grasped one of the bottom bed posts, yet she could see nothing. She recalled Roger Collins' warning that bolting her door would not protect her from the mansion's ghosts!

Victoria crouched in the bed in terror, sure that there was another presence in the dark room. Scarcely daring to breathe, she listened, wondering if she should leap from the bed and race to the bolted door, to the security of the corridor. But she was too frightened to move. There was a slight motion of the bed again, as if the unseen hand that had gripped the post had released it, and she heard what seemed a deep sigh. After that, there was nothing.

Too shocked to return to sleep, she lay in the bed listening. But there was only the wind and the occasional rattle of that loose shutter. After a long while her tension eased and she began to believe it must have all been her imagination. Once she had decided she'd heard the scraping noise, the sequence of the other frightening sounds had followed as a matter of course. She had created them in her terror. She must believe this if she was to stay in the old house.

Clutching to this faint belief, she managed to contain her fears and at last fell asleep again from sheer exhaustion. This time her rest was not disturbed. When she finally opened her eyes it was morning and bright sunlight was streaming in through the curtains of the casement window.

She remained in bed for a few minutes taking in the room. It seemed much pleasanter than it had on the previous night. The gray-patterned wallpaper was not bright, but it did show good taste. And the framed prints of clipper ships on the walls were in keeping with the atmosphere. Her eyes rested on the bedpost she had thought gripped by ghostly fingers in the night. The whole business seemed quite fantastic now, almost certainly the product of her too-active imagination. She quickly got up to wash and dress for breakfast.

When she left her room to go downstairs she noticed the door to young David's room was wide open. A glance showed her the rumpled bed was empty and so was the room. The boy had likely had breakfast and gone off somewhere.

Victoria made her way down the broad stairway to the foyer with its walnut-paneled walls and its portraits without encountering any other member of the household. She went into the dining room on the right and discovered a girl standing by a huge sideboard helping herself to food from a breakfast buffet. The girl must have heard her enter, for she at once turned around, plate in hand, a dazzling smile on her face.

"Hi!" she said. "You're Victoria! Mother told me you'd arrived, but I was late getting in and didn't like to bother you last night." She was a pretty girl with a marked resemblance to her mother. He lovely green eyes were her most notable attraction.

Victoria smiled. "And of course you're Carolyn."

"None other!" the seventeen-year-old girl said breezily. "Not Caroline the princess, nor Caroline the great, but just plain Caroline of this battered old house." She waved toward the sideboard with its spread of appetizing food. "Help yourself! We always have our meals buffet style. It's mother's answer to the servant problem."

"And a very practical one," she agreed, taking a glass and pouring herself orange juice from a pitcher.

"I suppose so," Carolyn agreed as she returned to sit at the long table with a plate of toast, bacon and eggs. "I have never thought of us as being practical. But then, I guess you're right. Mother is."

Victoria sat down across from the girl. "The sea looks

beautiful this morning. I'm looking forward to a stroll around the place. You must find it very exciting living here."

Carolyn's pretty young face took on an incredulous expression. "You can't really mean that! You're a New Yorker, Mother tells me, and I'd say that must be about the most exciting place on earth! Collinsport is deadly dull and Collins House is just plain creepy!"

"The New York I've known isn't so wonderful," Victoria assured her. "I worked in a foundling home."

Carolyn nodded, the large green eyes thoughtful. "Mother told me that. Anyway, I'm glad you're here. At least I'll have someone to talk to. I haven't had anyone near my own age for company since Mary Gordon left."

"The other governess."

"Yes," Carolyn said, a faint smile playing about her full lips. "I guess maybe you've heard about her."

"Not much. I gather she left rather hurriedly."

"You bet she did!" the other girl chuckled. "Poor Mary! Dealing with David wasn't enough. She had to cope with his father too!"

Victoria raised her eyebrows politely. "Oh?"

"Uncle Roger sometimes gets amorous when he's drinking," she warned. "Mary just couldn't take it any longer. Mother had the poor judgment to give her the room across the hall from him, but I see she's being more careful this time. Good job, too!"

"I haven't met David yet."

"He had breakfast and went out a little while ago. He's a regular little devil!"

Victoria laughed as she got up to help herself to some toast. "Well, at least nobody speaks too well of him."

"Neither will you, after you've sparred with him a week," Carolyn prophesied. "Do you frug?"

Victoria sat down with an amused expression. "No. And I can't do the Watusi either."

"I don't believe it!" the other girl exclaimed. "I thought everyone in New York was hep to the new dances!"

"We don't all spend our time at discotheques," Victoria told her. "All I can do is a plain two-step and some of the Latin dances."

"We do all the new dances down at the Blue Whale," Carolyn said happily. "That's a bar down off Main Street. They have a super jukebox and a lot of us kids gather there most every night."

"Sounds like a go-go swinging spot," Victoria said, secretly amused. She decided that Carolyn was secretly shy, but tried to put on a sophisticated manner to cover it up.

"It's a fun place and that's for sure," Carolyn agreed. "You'll have to come down with me. Of course, Mother won't approve, but don't let that stop you! What can you expect from someone who hasn't left this house for eighteen years?"

"I'm sure your mother must have a good reason for not leaving the estate," Victoria said quietly, not anxious to get involved in any family controversy.

Carolyn jumped up to go to the sideboard and pour herself a cup of coffee. Over her shoulder she said, "There's no such thing as a good reason for shutting yourself off from the world as she has." The girl brought her cup back to the table and sat down. "The trouble is, Mother sees herself as the grand lady of Collins House. We are all supposed to be her poor slaves and do her bidding. Probably that's why father ran off the way he did."

Victoria was desperately anxious to get off this subject. She said, "I had a near accident last night. Your cousin Ernest saved me."

"Mother told me," Carolyn said. "How do you like Ernest?"

"He seemed charming."

The other girl rolled her eyes. "You can say that again! Believe me, if we weren't related I'd set my cap for him!"

"He is a good deal older than you."

Carolyn shrugged. "So what? I like a mature man. Will Grant is another one I could really go for!"

Victoria smiled. "I've met him, too. He helped my cab driver fix a flat tire on our way here."

Carolyn looked impressed. "It seems to me you've met all the eligible men in the village and you've only been here less than twenty-four hours."

She laughed. "I promise I haven't tried to!"

"I know. You're one of those lucky gals! Men just drift your way! Wish I could join your company. But don't build any hopes on Will Grant. He's much too busy talking company affairs with Mother and looking after the sales quota to pay any attention to a pretty face. I know!"

Victoria gave her a teasing glance. "Keep trying. Sooner or later even the most staid male has to experience the great emotion."

Carolyn sighed and slumped back in her chair. "Ernest is a much better bet. He's really romantic, but then, most musicians are! And he has had one great love."

Victoria rose to get some coffee. "Aren't you afraid he'll come down and overhear you?" she said. "It could give him some kind of a complex."

"He went out even before David," Carolyn told her. "He's always out somewhere. I don't know when he ever sleeps. He prowls around day and night. Especially since all the trouble last year."

Trying to avoid any mention of the murder, Victoria merely

said, "He has a house of his own somewhere near here."

The other girl nodded. "You can see it from the left. It's about a half mile away on the left, a big yellow house with white columns on either side of the door. His grandfather built it, so it's not really as old as Collins House or as elaborate. But it is beautiful inside. It all belongs to Ernest now, since he's the last of his line. But I don't think he'll ever live there again. It reminds him of Elaine."

"Elaine?"

"She was his wife. I can remember when they lived at the house. She was a beauty and they entertained a lot. Mother didn't like her much. Thought she was too overbearing. I think that's funny coming from Mother, since she's so high and mighty herself. But Ernest was deeply in love with Elaine. She was a violinist, too, but not a top talent like Ernest. They met at the conservatory where he was teaching and she was his pupil."

"It sounds romantic," Victoria said, sipping her coffee.

Carolyn sighed. "It was. Mother claims they used to quarrel, but I don't believe it. Ernest and Elaine were madly in love and when she was killed in that auto accident near Los Angeles, he sort of fell apart."

"Was he in the car with her when it happened?"

"No. She was driving with a friend. Ernest was doing a concert in San Francisco. During the intermission they told him about the accident. He was hardly able to finish, although he didn't know right away how badly Elaine was injured. She lived on for nearly two weeks and then she died. He spent practically all that time at her bedside."

"Then he came back here?"

"No. He took a house on the ocean near Santa Barbara and lived alone for almost a year. He didn't play any concerts during those months. Then one spring night he drove back here. He arrived in the middle of the night and Mother let him in. I didn't see him until the next morning. When I did, I was shocked to see how thin he was and how much he'd aged."

Victoria said, "He looks well enough now."

"He's still far from being the old Ernest," the other girl said solemnly. "But those first weeks he was back, he acted real kookie! He closed up his own place and had Mother open up one of the sections on the upper floor that had been shut off for years and he lived there all by himself. He wouldn't even allow me to come and visit him there. After awhile he began to show interest in his violin again and started resuming concert engagements. He'd go away for a few days or a week but always come back here and lock himself up like a hermit or something."

"I suppose it was part of his readjustment," Victoria

suggested, pushing aside her empty cup.

"That's what Mother thinks," Carolyn said. "I'm not so sure. Sometimes I believe he went mad with grief at the shock of Elaine's death and he's still not quite sane."

Victoria looked startled. "That's a shocking statement," she told her.

Carolyn frowned. "I don't think I'm exaggerating. Ernest was quite different before he lost Elaine. He was never moody or grim as he so often is now. And he used to play gay tunes for me on his violin when I was a little girl. Now he rarely touches it unless he is preparing for a concert and then he rehearses only the numbers he is planning to play. I suppose he hates the violin because it reminds him of her and the way they used to play together."

"It must have been very difficult for him to return to his concert career."

"I'd say so," Carolyn agreed. "Last year I thought it all might change. There was this young artist who rented the extra cottage, a lovely blond girl from Boston. Ernest spent a lot of time in her company and he seemed almost his old self again." The girl paused awkwardly and stared down at the floor. She went on in a quieter tone, "One morning she was found dead on the rocks at low tide. She'd either fallen over or someone had pushed her. The police came and after a long time decided it had been an accident."

"I've heard something about it," Victoria admitted.

"Then you probably know they suspected Ernest might have been guilty of her murder for awhile," Carolyn said, looking at her with a sober expression. "It didn't matter that they vindicated him in the end. The harm had been done. All that he'd gained in knowing her was lost. He left here right away and I didn't think he'd be back. But he returned after a few months. It was then he left the apartment he'd made Mother open for him and took a room in the main section of the house with the rest of us. He seemed to have recovered from the second tragedy but there were still scars showing. Just as there are now."

Victoria said, "He's had a bad time. I hope the future holds better things for him."

"I wonder," Carolyn said wistfully. "I don't think he'll find happiness by remaining in this house. It's not here to find!" Victoria smiled faintly. "That's much too bitter a statement from someone as young as you are."

"I'm almost as old as you!" she said defiantly.

"But you haven't had to make your own way as I have."

"That doesn't mean it's been any easier," Carolyn argued. "I know you were raised in a foundling home, but I've never known a father. And I've had to live in this awful old place!" Victoria wondered how the girl knew so much about her. Elizabeth must have told her these things, and this confirmed her suspicions that Elizabeth knew more about her and those mysterious payments that had arrived monthly from Bangor than she was willing to let on. She was about to question the girl further when her mother entered the dining room.

Elizabeth looked less weary than on the previous night and was wearing a dark dress of smart cut. It was plain that she had not lost touch with fashion in her long sojourn in the old house. She offered them both a smile.

"I see you've already become acquainted," she said.

Carolyn rose and went across to her mother. "Yes. And I'd say you've chosen well this time," she said. "I like her."

Her mother nodded. "I was sure that you would." Turning to Victoria, she asked, "Did you have a good rest?"

"Once I got settled down," Victoria said. She would have liked to have told about the strange experience she'd had and how for a short while she'd been sure there was a weird presence in the room, but she knew her story would be discounted and she was no longer so certain herself that anything out of the ordinary had happened.

Elizabeth said, "It's a wonderful morning. Everyone is out except Roger and he hasn't even got up for breakfast yet."

"Not that there's anything new about that," Carolyn spoke up, wrinkling her pert nose in distaste.

Her mother chose to ignore this comment. She told Victoria, "I think you should also enjoy the air and sunshine while we have it. It's as warm as late August or September this morning. We do get these pet days in Maine all through October." Carolyn smiled at Victoria. "I'll go with you, if you like."

Victoria had already risen from the table. "I'd enjoy that."

"I'm sorry," Elizabeth said sharply. "I need you here for awhile, Carolyn. I have a few things to discuss with you. Especially what kept you so late at the Blue Whale last night." "Joe Haskell wanted to stay late and dance," Carolyn said plaintively. "Can't we talk about it later?"

"I'm afraid not," her mother said, her determination apparent in the handsome face so lightly touched by time. "You go ahead, Miss Winters. Perhaps after I've talked with Carolyn she'll catch up with you."

"Of course," Victoria said. "I plan to stroll toward the cliff." She left the two in the dining room and made her way to the front door and out to the steps. She stood there a moment, gazing across the wide lawns that extended as far as the cliff. Beyond was the ocean, placid on this lovely morning, a rippling pattern of silver under the bright sun.

She was of the opinion Elizabeth had a double reason for not allowing her daughter to join her in her stroll. No doubt she did want to reprimand her for remaining out so late the previous night, but Victoria was also sure that the older woman wanted to take this opportunity of warning Carolyn not to talk too much, not to reveal any of their carefully guarded secrets to her. It wasn't a pleasant conclusion, but she felt it to be the truth.

The cab driver had been right when he'd told her the grounds were no longer kept up properly. They were in poor shape. Evidently Matt Morgan kept the lawns directly in front of the entrance cut, but at the sides the grass was now tall and what had once been neat hedges had grown wildly. All in all the neglect was depressing and reflected on the state of mind of the occupants of Collins House.

There was no question of their having the money to spend on upkeep. The Collins family was the wealthiest in the area and the fish cannery was apparently growing all the time.

Elizabeth had deliberately dismissed all the household help the day after her husband vanished. Since then Morgan had been the only servant allowed to remain on the grounds.

Why had Elizabeth sent the servants away? What had really happened to her husband? What had made her become a recluse, unwilling to leave the estate for years on end? Victoria was certain if she knew the answers to these questions she would be much closer to the secret of Collins House and perhaps nearer the answer to the mystery of her own beginnings. She strolled along the gravel driveway, occupied with these tormenting thoughts.

She passed a large masonry flowerpot that had a big chip off one side and a giant crack in the other. Instead of flowers it was filled with weeds. It seemed no one cared—just as no one took any interest in the hedge to her right that had grown in a fantastic, uneven fashion. As she gazed at the green hedge with troubled eyes, she became aware of a slight movement behind it. She at once realized someone had taken a stand there to spy on her. It came as a shock.

Summoning her courage, she said in a clear, firm voice, "I know there is someone concealed there. You may as well come out." For a moment nothing happened. Bluffing, she added, "I know who it is. So you may as well show yourself."

There was a long interval of silence and not a hint of motion from the hedge until all at once there was a scurrying and the bushes trembled as the unknown watcher attempted to flee. Victoria had expected this. She also ran at exactly the same moment and headed directly toward the end of the hedge. She arrived there breathless but in time to cut off the escape of the one who had been spying on her.

He stood there crouched and ready to dart right or left as she faced him. There was no question in her mind that the small, wiry figure with the impassive young face was David Collins.

She said, "You weren't fast enough to get away!"

"Smart!" he said, in a sneering tone. It was the kind of reply she might have expected from an adult and it was the first hint she had of the boy's character.

"I'm Victoria Winters, your new governess," she said.

"You won't last long!" He was all defiance.

"Is that why you were spying on me? Why you ran away when I spoke to you? Have you made up your mind I'm your enemy before you even know me?"

He studied her uneasily. "You're like the rest of them! I don't want you or any other old governess. I want my mother back!"

In spite of his hostility these last words touched her deeply. At once she felt a tenderness for the boy. It was not hard to understand why he was so unhappy and hated the substitute mothers his father and aunt had foisted on him.

She spoke quickly. "I'm sorry about your mother. And when I have a chance I'll speak to your father and ask about when she's coming back. Does that satisfy you?"

"You're lying," he said. "Why should you care?"

"But I do!" she protested. "I want to be your friend!"

He answered with a mocking peal of childish laughter and then he darted by her to vanish behind the shelter of some distant hedges. She watched him go, a frustrated expression on her attractive face. She and her charge had met for the first time and it hadn't gone too well.

She resumed her stroll toward the cliff in a more somber mood. All the stories she had been told about the boy had been only too true. It was not going to be easy to win his confidence and affection. It might even be impossible.

At least one gain had come out of her meeting with the lad. He had allowed the true cause of his rebellious attitude to slip out. He missed his mother! With this knowledge to help her she might manage some headway with him. She would begin by consulting his father, then Elizabeth Stoddard, if she received no cooperation from the boy's parent. She wanted to know why the boy had been separated from his mother and whether the parting was to be a permanent one. It was another of the mysteries of Collins House which she must try to solve.

The air had a salt tang as she came to the footpath that followed the sheer cliff overlooking the sea. There was a slight wind, the last remnant of the previous night's storm, but she did not feel cold; she'd thrown her trench coat over her shoulders as a buffer against it. Far out to sea she saw a freighter making its way lazily along the horizon, a sooty spiral wafting up from its single funnel.

Below her the waves dashed angrily on the jagged rocks, leaving a wake of white foam after every assault. She continued on toward the highest point of the cliff and here paused to look back at the gloomy hulk of Collins House standing darkly against the clear blue sky, its chimneys reaching up like thin black tentacles, its captain's walk bleak and deserted. She allowed her eyes to wander down the coast and about a mile distant she saw the large yellow mansion that must belong to Ernest Collins. It struck her that it was not nearly so forbidding as the older house.

"Enjoying the view, Miss Winters?" The tone was light and the voice familiar.

Victoria turned and found herself facing an amused Ernest Collins. The concert violinist was wearing dark brown trousers and a heavy, beige turtleneck sweater. Except for the pallor of his sensitive face he look every inch the country squire.

She said, "It is a beautiful spot."

"I agree," he said. "But it has a sad history."

"In what way?"

"You know that it's called Widow's Hill. But I hardly imagine you've been here long enough to discover how it came by its name."

"That's true," she said, feeling a little easier. For a moment she had thought he was going to mention the suicide of the young artist last summer.

"Long before Jeremiah Collins built his mansion here, this was a sort of common gathering ground," he explained, staring out at the ocean. "In those days all the men of the village were fishermen and they would put out to sea for their catch and remain away often for days at a time. Often storms would come up unexpectedly and since this was the highest point of land, their wives would come up here and watch anxiously for the boats to return." He paused. "Only too often they never did come back to Collinsport. And it was on this very hill that the wives realized it had come their turn to be widows. Many tears have been shed on this very point of land."

"It's a sad story," Victoria said.

"It has an even more melancholy ending," Ernest assured her. "When Jeremiah bought the land he refused to let any of the townspeople use it and so the waiting wives would come here no more. They cursed my ancestor and wished bad luck on all his kin. It seems the curse had power. None of the family have been happy here. First to suffer was Josette, the French bride for whom Jeremiah built Collins House. She threw herself from this cliff, down the full hundred feet to her death. And there have been others since then."

Victoria regarded him skeptically. "But can you really be superstitious enough to believe in such a thing as an ancient curse?"

The handsome man shrugged. "I wonder. When I think

of Elizabeth a prisoner of this place for eighteen years by her own wish, Roger slowly drinking himself to death, and Carolyn restless and unhappy and almost sure to involve herself in some youthful tragedy"—he paused with a grim smile—"not to mention myself or poor little David. You are a brave girl to take your place among us."

"Now you're being deliberately melodramatic," she said with a faint smile. "You are painting the picture darker than it should be."

"It could be that I'm sparing you the worst details," he said soberly, his eyes fixed on her with a burning intensity.

The strangeness of his gaze and the tragic tone in which he spoke sent a tremor of uneasiness through her. She found herself thinking of his near collapse when his wife died as the result of the car accident and the grisly business of the artist's mysterious fall from where they were standing.

She forced herself to meet his gaze and in a soft voice inquired, "Are you deliberately trying to scare me away?"

He was silent for a moment. Then he shook his head. "No," he said. "No. I don't want to do that. You have courage. That's apparent. And you have youth and brightness as well. We can use some of that here. Especially the boy."

"I know," she said. "I've been admiring your house. Do you intend to open it again?"

He glanced in the direction of the big yellow and white house. "No," he said, his voice oddly harsh. "That part of my life is over. The happiness I knew there once can never be recaptured. It would be a mockery for me to try and recover any of it."

Victoria felt rebuffed. And she was moved by the tragic expression on his lean, handsome face. She could sense the deep sorrow that memories of the good days in that other mansion had brought him, and she found herself despairing of Ernest Collins' ever regaining even a semblance of happiness. His love for Elaine must have been such a special thing, the link between them so perfect and so strong, that the wrench of her death had left him scarred and incomplete. No, it was not likely Ernest Collins would ever love another as he had loved his beautiful lost Elaine.

She said, "I'm sorry I asked such a stupid question. Forgive me."

At once his manner changed and he became apologetic. "It is I who should be sorry," he said. "That was a stupid display of self-pity. I'd hoped I'd gotten past that stage."

Victoria said, "I'm glad you're playing again. Your music has meant so much to millions of people. You should never desert your violin."

He offered her a sad smile. "It's not likely to happen. It is the main thing left to me. I—" He suddenly broke off in midsentence and stared in shocked silence at Collins House.

Victoria automatically turned to look and see what had caught his attention. It was the slim silhouette of a woman standing alone in the captain's walk atop the gloomy mansion, apparently watching them. The distance was too great to make out who it was. She glanced at Ernest. "There's someone watching us up there!"

He gave her a guilty look and shook his head. "No. There's no one up there."

Victoria turned to look again. Whoever had been there had quickly disappeared. She appealed to him now with a troubled expression. "But there was someone there only a moment ago!" she protested.

"No!" he said, almost angrily. "There was no one!" He hurried off in the direction of the house, leaving her standing there in confusion.

CHAPTER 4

Victoria stood watching his rapidly retreating form as he continued on his way to the great dark mansion. Ernest Collins' strange behavior was beyond understanding. She drew her coat close around her as a chill made her tremble slightly. It was not the cool wind that caused her to feel this way, but the terror of the unknown. In this frightening interlude with the concert violinist, all her apprehensions had returned.

The waves crashed relentlessly against the rocks below and the sound filled her with new despair and loneliness. She saw Ernest enter the house by the main door.

Whom had he seen on the captain's walk? Why had he deliberately lied to her, claiming there had been no one up there, when she had seen the woman watching them? It had been a weird sort of phantom figure and like a phantom it had vanished in a twinkling. Yet Victoria knew it was no ghost they had seen, but a flesh-and-blood member of the strange household. There were no women servants, so it had to be either Elizabeth or her daughter, Carolyn. But why should Ernest behave so strangely at the sight?

It was only then that a third and startling possibility came to her. Might it not have been Roger Collins' missing wife? Could it be that she was secretly a resident in the sprawling old mansion? Was there some reason why she was concealing herself this way? The thought made Victoria all the more determined to speak to Roger at the first opportunity and ask for the truth about his absent wife.

No longer interested in her walk, she decided to go directly back to the house. It was likely Roger Collins would be up by now and she might have a chance to talk to him. She retraced her steps along the narrow path and made her way to the front door.

She had almost reached the steps when she saw something that caused her to pause and then stroll toward the east wing where she'd been heading the previous evening when Ernest saved her from the hazard of the rotten well covering. Elizabeth had told her the wing had been closed for years and the side door was never used. Now it was partly ajar!

Filled with curiosity, Victoria advanced toward it. As she did so, she walked along a flagstone path that led past the planked square covering an ancient well. She saw how close she had come to stepping on its treacherous surface the night before and understood clearly why Ernest had moved so quickly to her rescue. What she found more difficult to understand was why it had not been repaired since it presented danger to the family, as well as to any strangers who happened by. But then, its neglect was in accord with the other examples of laxness she had seen about the place.

As she came close to the door with its dusty glass panes and old-fashioned padlock that had only so recently been opened, she hesitated a moment. Her eyes moved to the ground-level windows of the shut-off wing and as she glanced from one to the other she was abruptly confronted with a strange sight that froze her where she stood. Her eyes went wide as she saw the shadow of a slight figure press close to the yellowed curtains and stare out at her. Then the curtain flicked and the shadow of the thin head and shoulders vanished as quickly as it had appeared. Coming so close after her other experience, it made her wonder if she wasn't beginning to see things.

But in the same instant she told herself this was no illusion. There had been someone in that window, but whether it was a man or woman she could not say. It could even have been David, though she had no idea how he could have found his way into the locked wing. Well, of course, she reminded herself sharply. He could have walked in through the open door that was only a few feet away from her.

This brought up the question of who had left the door ajar and why? She decided she would find out for herself and with some hesitation advanced to the side entry. She paused at the worn stoop and pushed the door open a little further. It creaked rustily and she was assailed by the damp stench found in most old buildings that have been closed for long periods.

Ahead of her was a second battered door of solid wood, painted a dark green and also ajar. Beyond that was darkness. Victoria stepped inside. She touched her hand to the inner door to swing it open, she was violently flung back by someone else—a giant of a man in rough working clothes. He had an ugly face and he was glaring down at her.

"Who are you?" she gasped.

"Morgan," he said in a rough voice. "You got no right to be in here!"

"I saw the door open," she faltered.

"Mrs. Elizabeth's orders," Morgan said stubbornly. "No one allowed in the east wing."

"But someone is in there," she said. "I saw a head and shoulders in one of the windows."

He towered above her, a scornful expression on his slab face. "You're wrong about that," he said. "No one in here!" She glanced beyond him at the stench-ridden darkness and felt certain he was lying. "But I saw someone. I know I did. And you were in there."

"Break in the water pipes. They run under here and I had to fix it," he said. "Now I'm ready to lock up again."

"So you won't let me in then?"

"No one is allowed, like I said," he told her stubbornly. "Everything is rotted out and dangerous. Mrs. Elizabeth don't want any accidents, so she gives orders for no one to ever go in." He showed no sign of budging.

Victoria realized it was hopeless. Matt Morgan was apparently doggedly faithful to Mrs. Stoddard and had no intention of defying her orders. She would do better to present her story directly to the mistress of Collins House and see her reaction.

Retreating a step, she said, "Very well, Morgan. I'll speak to Mrs. Stoddard about what's happened."

The big man scowled. "If you're planning to make a complaint against me, you best save your time. It won't do any good." And he busied himself fitting the padlock back in place on the inner door.

Victoria went out into the sunshine again. It was a relief to fill her lungs after standing in the shaded vestibule with its fetid air. She made her way to the main entrance and mounted the steps and went inside. There was no sign of Elizabeth, but Roger Collins came to the doorway of the dining room and regarded her with a smile.

"Miss Winters," he said, "Miss Victoria Winters, isn't it? My recollections of last night are none too clear." He accompanied this statement with a knowing wink.

"That's right," she agreed, slipping off her coat and remembering he was the one she had originally started back to the house to question. Now she was more anxious to talk with his sister.

"Then I may call you Victoria, I hope," he said in an ingratiating manner. "I don't believe in stiff formality. And you shall call me Roger."

"If you like," she said quietly, knowing that her dislike for the weakly handsome Roger was as deep-rooted and primitive as her feeling of sympathy for Ernest. It was a question of instinct, something over which she had no control.

"I'm glad to have that settled, Victoria," he said, beaming at her. "I know we'll get along just fine. Nothing cheers me like a pretty face."

"But it's not my face that brought me here," she reminded him with some tartness. "Rather the fact that I happen to be a teacher."

Roger looked slightly surprised at this rebuff. "Naturally," he said in his smooth way. "And I'm happy to have you here in that capacity. My boy is badly in need of help."

"I couldn't agree more," Victoria said, looking at him with a stern expression on her pretty face.

It was apparent that her manner was making him wary. He said, "Then you have already met David."

"We had a brief meeting in the garden," she said.

"He's a smart youngster. But badly mixed up."

"So I discovered. And I must say I think most of the blame is yours."

"Mine!" Roger exclaimed.

She nodded. "Yes. It's stupid to blame the boy. I feel his chief problem is his insecure feeling and that comes as a result of his being taken from his mother."

Roger's almost-handsome face flushed. "Am I to understand that you were able to come to this remarkable conclusion as the result of a short meeting in the garden with the boy? You must indeed be a crack psychiatrist! Your services should be in demand!"

It was her turn to feel her cheeks burn. She forced herself to keep her temper and reply quietly. "I make no such claim," she said. "But David did reveal some of his inner thinking without realizing it."

Roger smiled nastily. "I'll be a lot more pleased if you'll confine your efforts to teaching the boy arithmetic and spelling and refrain from psychoanalyzing him!"

"Then you don't think his state of mind important?"

"Very important. I leave it in your competent care, Victoria."

"I can't promise anything unless I know something about his problem. Something about his missing mother."

"It seems to me you have a complex about missing parents."

"Having one of your usual arguments, Roger?" Elizabeth had joined them by way of the corridor leading from the rear of the mansion. She stood studying her younger brother icily.

"Victoria and I were coming to an understanding," he said with a forced smile. "No harm done."

"How unlike you to quarrel with a pretty girl," Elizabeth told him. "Or has Victoria already let you know she is impervious to your dubious charm?" She paused. "I should think Burke Devlin's being back here would be enough to keep your mind occupied these days."

Roger's face went pale. "Let's leave Burke Devlin out of this," he said.

"Then I suggest you watch your behavior." Elizabeth turned to Victoria. "You seem to have a knack for involving yourself in trouble, Miss Winters. Morgan has come to me with a tale that you tried to threaten him."

"That's idiotic!" Victoria said. "I saw the door of the old wing open and went inside. He refused to let me past the inner door and claimed it was on your orders."

"That's true. The old wing is in bad repair. Not safe for visitors."

"But I saw someone in it. A face at one of the windows."

Elizabeth offered her a glacial smile. "Come, Miss Winters. That is quite impossible."

Victoria regarded her defiantly. "I have never been accused of seeing things until I came here. I did see the face, even though you deny it. And earlier I saw a figure upon the captain's walk. Your cousin was with me at the time; we were standing on the cliff. And he said I was mistaken. Is this some sort of insane joke you're all playing on me?"

Elizabeth was at once placating. "You need have no fear of that. I can't offer any explanation of the face you saw in the window, other than your own imagination. But I can clear your mind concerning the figure up on the captain's walk. It was I. I saw you two standing on the cliff. I was only there for a moment and perhaps Ernest didn't notice me."

"But I'm sure he did," Victoria protested. "He saw you even before I did and then, for some strange reason, he denied it." Elizabeth showed concern. "I believe I can also explain why he behaved so oddly."

"Really?"

"Yes." The older woman paused and sighed. "In spite of the remarkable recovery he's made from the depression he sank into after his wife's death, he is still not what could be termed normal mentally."

"He seems sane enough to me," she said. "And he has

resumed his career."

"That is so," Elizabeth agreed. "And I am so thankful that he has so nearly recovered. But he does have minor regressions. The instance of which you speak probably is an example." She hesitated. "The young woman who fell to her death from the cliff last year was an artist. She and Ernest were very close. It is my belief he may have been in love with her. This young woman often went up to the captain's walk to do a painting of the view from there."

Victoria frowned. "I still don't see the connection between that and why he behaved so oddly when he saw you."

"It's simple enough when you understand the confused state of his mind," the older woman said quietly. "Ernest mistook me for the ghost of that girl!"

"I can't accept that!" Victoria protested.

"You may later, when you see more of my cousin," Elizabeth said. "I have taken your word for his behavior and I'm merely trying to offer a logical explanation as I see it."

"I'm sorry," Victoria told her. "I'm still not satisfied." But the woman had upset her. What Elizabeth said might be true. If it was, then she couldn't put aside the suspicion that Ernest might be a murderer after all—a murderer who had evaded punishment, but who now went to pieces when he saw what he believed to be the ghost of the girl he had sent hurtling down on those jagged rocks. It fitted!

Elizabeth was still facing her. Now she said, "What was your difficulty with Roger?"

"I told him I thought David is like he is because he misses his mother. I asked whether there was any good reason for his not seeing her."

The older woman frowned slightly. "You shouldn't have said that."

"But the boy's emotional troubles must be settled before he can be expected to behave in a normal fashion or even settle down to his studies."

"I appreciate your solicitude," Elizabeth said coldly. "But you need only concern yourself with teaching him."

"Will his mother ever come back?"

"I can not answer your question," the mistress of Collins House said with a touch of annoyance. "Neither can Roger. It is useless to keep harping on it. Frankly, it is none of your business."

"But I promised David I would ask his father," she protested. "I thought he might be pleased and it would help me reach the boy."

"You are quite wrong in that," Elizabeth declared emphatically. "You are in no position to find answers for him. I count on you not to torment him with false hopes and to concentrate on your role as teacher. Incidentally, you'll find all his lesson books and Miss Gordon's notes on the desk in the library. I found them and left them out for you. Perhaps you should take a look at them now. It's the last door down on the left."

Victoria knew she was being curtly dismissed, but there was nothing she could do but accept with good grace. She said, "Thank you. I'll glance through them at once." And she went down the hall to the library.

The library was as richly furnished as the other rooms in the main section of the house. Three of its walls were lined with books from floor to ceiling. The other wall was given to a huge fireplace over which hung a painting by some long-dead artist, showing Collins House as it looked in the early part of the nineteenth century.

Victoria was in such a melancholy mood that she paid little attention to it, sitting down at the wide mahogany desk, she began to systematically go over the text books and loose-leaf lesson books belonging to young David. It didn't take her long to learn that he was apparently extremely intelligent and well ahead in his studies for his age. She derived some small satisfaction from this discovery and began to plan how she would begin his new study sessions.

Still rankling her was the scene she'd had with his father. And she was not satisfied with Elizabeth's attitude, either. She could understand their strong dislike of the boy's mother if she had deserted Roger and the youngster, but surely they could have simply admitted this, without making such a fuss and creating what amounted to a mystery over her absence.

It seemed that even the single servant at Collins House had become infected with the tight-lipped surliness characteristic of the family. Once again Victoria had a strong impulse to admit defeat and pack her suitcases and return to New York. The villagers who had warned her about the old house on Widow's Hill had not exaggerated the situation. In some ways it was even worse than they had pictured it.

But her desire to find out if there was any link between these people and her own past was still strong, and she was sincerely concerned about David's welfare. For these reasons she was determined to stay. And perhaps there was an interest in Ernest Collins, a sympathy for the sensitive musician which she would not dare admit. Not when it was possible he had committed a murder.

She had been tired and jittery ever since arriving at Collins House. The journey had been a long and difficult one and the storm had not helped. Her troubles had continued during the cab trip from the village and only the timely appearance of the pleasant Will Grant had prevented her from spending all or at least a good part of the night in the broken down taxi. The remembrance of the helpful young lawyer gave her some comfort.

He had spoken as if he visited Collins House regularly and said she could expect to see him soon again. She hoped it would work out that way; it would give her someone to tell her troubles to. At least he would offer her a link with the normal world. Here there were only a collection of neurotics, with the possible exception of Carolyn.

The pretty seventeen-year-old had impressed her. But even she showed the strain of having been brought up in this tense atmosphere. Carolyn was bursting to get away from the bleak mansion and see something of life in the everyday world. This urge for freedom had grown to such proportions with her that Victoria feared she was regarding the outside world with too romantic a vision. The girl might wake up one day to discover that the world's unhappiness was not confined to this old house. It was just that the tensions and hatreds were more concentrated here.

"Hi, teacher!" It was Carolyn who now poked her head in the door of the library. "Can I join your class?"

Victoria managed a smile. "If you like."

Carolyn came in. "I've been wandering around upstairs looking for you. It's almost lunch time and I wanted to have a chat." She gave a sigh and glanced toward the door. "Mother read me the riot act about being out so late and says I can't go with Joe Haskell anymore. She also says I can't go to town on my own."

"She'll probably forget about her new rules later."

"Maybe," Carolyn said. "But I don't count on it. So what good is having my own car if I can't go anywhere? That's why I wanted to talk to you."

Victoria sat back from the books and eyed the girl. "I'm willing to listen, although I'm sure I don't know how I can help."

"That's easy," Carolyn said slyly. "You can come into the village with me. Mother won't dare object as long as I have you for a chaperone."

"Don't be too sure. Anyway, I doubt that I'd enjoy the Blue Whale."

"It's not bad. And the drug store stays open until nine-thirty. You can always tell mother you've something to pick up there."

"In other words, lie to your mother. That could end with my being in more trouble than I am now."

Carolyn showed surprise. "What trouble are you in now?" She leaned forward.

"Your Uncle Roger and I had some words," Victoria said with a sigh. "It concerned David." And she went on to explain.

"You're probably right," Carolyn agreed with a small frown. "But I can understand Uncle Roger being upset. It's a touchy subject with him."

"Surely one is allowed to mention that he has a wife?"

"Roger is unhappy about his marriage. But he'll likely apologize to you."

"What about Burke Devlin? Your mother mentioned him to your uncle and it seemed to upset him badly. Why? Who is Burke Devlin?"

Carolyn sighed. "Mother does that deliberately when she wants to annoy Roger. For some reason he and Burke Devlin are enemies. Burke is a fascinating man who used to live here once. He came back awhile ago and he seems to be very rich."

"Has he some business here?"

"I can't tell you," Carolyn said. "There are a lot of rumors. I think he's just a wealthy, retired eccentric. And Roger is not a bad man, though he can be difficult."

Victoria gave a small shrug. "I haven't formed any definite opinions as to whether he's good or bad. But I do think he's dangerously neglectful of his young son."

"And he drinks too much," Carolyn said with resignation. "And mother considers him a woman-chaser. Yet if he weren't my uncle and older I'm sure I'd find him fascinating."

Victoria raised her eyebrows. "I'm not so impressed," she said.

A mischievous gleam showed in the teenager's eyes. She said, "I guess you find Cousin Ernest a lot more romantic."

The teasing remark caused Victoria to blush furiously. "I don't know why you think that," she said. "He's very nice, but I've had very little time to really get to know him."

"But you do like him."

"He's a talented, sensitive man and I owe him a debt for rescuing me from possible danger."

"Ernest is a very different type from Uncle Roger," Carolyn said.

"That's obvious."

"I don't think you know what I mean," the girl said. "He's very deep. He keeps things to himself. Ernest is not easy to understand or know well."

Remembering the peculiar incident on the cliff, Victoria could not argue. "I realize that," she said quietly.

Carolyn stood up. "Don't think I want to interfere. But I'd go slow with Cousin Ernest if I were you. He isn't quite what he seems to be." She remained standing there in silence for a second, a troubled look on her pretty face, as if there was something else she was about to say. Then she seemed to change her mind. Without uttering another word, she turned and quickly left the library.

It was another of those puzzling moments that had plagued Victoria since her entrance into the strange household. She wondered why the girl was trying to warn her against entering into too close a friendship with her cousin. No doubt she had vivid memories of that other girl in whom he'd showed an interest last summer and the tragedy that had brought the friendship to an abrupt end. It could even be that Carolyn knew more about the young artist's plunge over the cliff than she dared divulge! It was a frightening possibility.

She did her best to put the conversation out of her mind and went back to David's exercise books. She was still busy with this task when Roger Collins presented himself in the doorway of the library. As his niece had predicted, his mood had mellowed and he now wore an apologetic smile.

"Surely you're going to take time off for luncheon, Victoria," he said in his most genial fashion. "The others are all gathered in the dining room and Elizabeth asked me to try and locate you."

She closed the book she'd been studying and glanced up at him with a smile. "Thank you. I hadn't realized it was so late. And I'm not acquainted with the routine of the household yet."

"Elizabeth prefers that we have luncheon at twelve-thirty and she is rather particular about our being on time. It helps her since she has to prepare all the meals on her own."

"I can understand that," Victoria said, getting up from the chair. "I don't know how she manages to keep this big house so clean and do all the kitchen chores as well."

"It's her own choice," Roger said with a wry expression. "And the house is not all that tidy. You'll find plenty of dust around if you look closely enough." He paused. "But Elizabeth is not the only peculiar one here. We all have our quirks. I'm afraid I showed some of mine this morning."

Victoria raised an eyebrow. "I wasn't aware of it."

He looked amused. "Don't try to be polite. I certainly wasn't when you questioned me about David's mother."

"I didn't mean to intrude on your privacy."

"I see that now," he agreed. "I'm sorry I didn't then. It's a subject still very painful to me. When I am able to talk about it, I'll give you the full details. Until then I must ask you to be patient and do the best you can for my boy."

"You can be sure of that," she told him quietly. Gesturing toward the books grouped on the desk, she added, "He is remarkably intelligent. I'm looking forward to working with him."

Roger's weakly handsome face showed appreciation of this compliment. "Fine," he said. "Though I'm sure he doesn't inherit his brains from me. Elizabeth never neglects to remind me if I hadn't inherited a position with the company I would be unemployable."

Victoria smiled. "Brothers are rarely appreciated."

"Now that's a kind remark," Roger said, beaming at her as he escorted her to the hallway. "I can see that you are a truly understanding person, Victoria. I know we'll become close friends." He grasped her arm in much too familiar a way and to her embarrassment made no move to release her as they neared the dining room.

Luncheon was fairly pleasant. Elizabeth Stoddard dominated the gathering at the long dining table. She spent a good deal of the time giving Victoria a history of the village and painted an interesting picture of it in the early days. Her stories of clipper ships with their cargoes of aromatic teas, exotic spices and gleaming ivory held Victoria enchanted.

Roger and his cousin Ernest added little to the conversation, seeming content to listen, while Carolyn was as enthralled by her mother's stories as was Victoria. David was not at the table. She was told he'd eaten earlier and gone across to Matt Morgan's cottage. It seemed he spent a good deal of his free time in the gardener's company.

Near the end of the luncheon Carolyn burst out, "You make the old Collinsport sound so enchanting, Mother! I wish I had lived here then and not now when there's nothing more exciting than drinking canned beer and dancing the Watusi in the Blue Whale!"

Roger Collins chuckled. "Don't be carried away by Elizabeth's glamorizing the past, my dear. It wasn't all majestic ships and pretty frills and laces."

There was an awkward moment of silence at the table. Elizabeth sat very straight in her most aristocratic manner, a faintly annoyed expression on the still lovely face.

She spoke sharply, "Must you always be so cynical, Roger?"

He spread his hands. "It has to do with truth, not cynicism." He glanced across the table to Ernest for support. "Don't you agree that Elizabeth was offering us a pleasant fable rather than a true picture of the era?"

"I don't pretend to be an authority," Ernest said quietly. Roger smiled arrogantly and turned to Victoria. "There was a darker side to the old days that Eilzabeth seems to prefer not to mention. There was the fetid stench of hundreds of slaves cooped up in the holds of some of those ships like so many animals. There was the cruelty and indifference to the suffering poor, and there was the dark shadow of madness as well. The history of the Collins family should include all these if it is to be faithful to the truth."

From the head of the table there came an indignant gasp from Elizabeth. "You're talking nonsense, Roger! What will Victoria think of us? I do not know of any Collins who was in the slave trade, nor can I recall any instances of cruelty in our history, nor any insistent strain of madness!"

Roger regarded his sister blandly. "I'm sorry, Elizabeth, I must disagree. The early records of our vessels show that some were leased to known slavers and surely that represented indifference to suffering. As for the madness, there were recorded cases—which is true if you study almost any family history." Now he turned his gaze directly on the troubled face of Ernest Collins, who had suddenly gone pale. "And it wouldn't surprise me if actual cases of insanity could be found in our present generation."

This extraordinary statement again brought shocked silence. Ernest Collins rose from the table suddenly and marched out of the dining room.

CHAPTER 5

Victoria tried hard to conceal how disconcerted she was. Ernest's revealing reaction to Roger's pointed remark had shocked her. Indeed, all the others at the long table seemed to share her startled feelings. All except Roger, who sipped his coffee casually, looking smug.

Elizabeth gave her younger brother an angry glance and then abruptly began a discussion with Carolyn about the weekly grocery shopping, which the girl apparently took care of in the nearby town of Ellsworth, which had a large supermarket and shopping center. The luncheon ended on a casual note, as it had begun.

Roger vanished upstairs almost at once. Victoria was of the opinion that he had probably gone up to help himself to an after-meal drink. Elizabeth and Carolyn went down the hallway to the rear of the mansion, still discussing their shopping needs. Victoria found herself alone in the foyer.

For a moment she turned her attention to a large painting of a clipper ship in full sail. It seemed incongruous to imagine that the hold of the proud, beautiful ship should contain a cargo of closely-pressed, sweating black bodies, yet the wealth of many an otherwise respectable family was built on the proceeds of that foul trade. Roger had certainly hit on a touchy point when he'd brought out this fact. But she thought he had gone too far in directing his comments about family madness toward Ernest. She could not blame the young violinist for leaving the table as he had. What had induced Roger to make such a statement? Was he speaking from a certain knowledge or was he merely stabbing in the dark because he still suspected that Ernest might have murdered that girl last summer?

She felt an overwhelming desire to get out of the shadowed old house with its veiled feuds and tensions. No wonder young Carolyn was anxious to escape its drab atmosphere or that the boy, David, was twisted by the environment which surrounded him. She grasped the wrought iron knob of the great oak door and swung it open.

The cool breeze outdoors was refreshing and the warm sunshine encouraged her to descend the wide stone steps and stroll across the lawn. She was soon faced with the tall, untrimmed hedges. She heard the crunch of footsteps on the gravel walk ahead of her and a moment later rounded a tall screen of bushes to find herself in the company of Ernest Collins.

The violinist smiled wryly at her. "I didn't expect you to follow me."

"I didn't," she protested, slightly flustered.

"I'm glad you did come out this way, whatever the reason," he said, turning his handsome face toward the sea so that the sun's rays shone on him directly, revealing the deeply-etched lines of sorrow and the general sadness of his expression. "I've been standing here with only my thoughts for company and I assure you they are not such pleasant thoughts."

Victoria frowned slightly. "I don't know what could have gotten into Roger, to make him talk so wildly at the table."

"He enjoys being the center of attention," Ernest said with a grim smile. "He'll say anything for shock value."

"Not a very pleasant trait."

"I'll be glad to get away," Ernest said, glancing her way again. "I'll be leaving tomorrow and staying away a week. I'm giving some concerts in the Midwest."

"Wonderful! It will do you good to leave here."

"I suppose so—though concerts don't interest me as they used to."

"I can't believe it is healthy for you in this place. Nor for any of the rest of them, either. But you are free to live anywhere you like."

He sighed. "Perhaps not as free as you imagine."

She saw the new shadow cross his face and searched her mind for words to lighten his humor. In desperation, she asked, "What numbers are you doing on your tour?"

Ernest smiled. "You're not really interested, are you?"

"But of course I am. I'd very much like to know."

His eyes narrowed with pleasant disbelief as he stared at her under the blazing sun. "How long it has been since anyone has shown that enthusiasm about the concerts," he said quietly.

"Do you ever play anything by Prokofiev?" Victoria wanted to know.

"I sometimes do the first violin concerto," he said with a smile. "But not this time."

"Do you select your own programs?"

"Yes. Unless I have some special requests. One of the items in my concert this time will be Barber's violin concerto and I'm doing selections by Vivaldi, Bach and Brahms."

Victoria's eyes were bright with interest. "I've enjoyed your records. I'd like to hear you play in person some time."

He laughed lightly. "If you strain your ears you'll be able to do that this afternoon. I'll be running over my program in my room a little later on."

"It must be wonderful to have so much talent," she said.

"And boring at times," he said with a twinkle in his eyes. "Every so often I feel like really shocking my audience by playing my own interpretation of some pleasant, trivial show tune."

Victoria was amused by this. "I'm sure it would be interesting."

"What composers do you like? Are you acquainted with Mahler's symphonies?"

She nodded excitedly. "He's just recently become one of my enthusiasms. How many symphonies did he write? About ten?"

"And all good ones," Ernest agreed. "You really are a music buff!"

"Everyone knows Mahler," she protested.

"Not by any means." he said.

They talked on for several minutes matching enthusiasms and generally exploring the world of music and musicians. Victoria had spent many evenings alone in her room at the foundling home listening to concerts on her FM set. She'd been given permission to use it at night, providing she kept the volume down. Now the many hours spent with her ear against the modest set were paying her an extra dividend.

Ernest Collins had changed during their excited discussion and now seemed a much different person. His face had lost its weary look and grown animated. "It's been great talking to you this way," he said. "We must do more of it when I come back."

"I'll look forward to that," Victoria said with a touch of shyness. She had met few men with the compelling personality of Ernest Collins. But in addition to seeming very worldly, he was still nearly a stranger. Although she had been drawn to him from the first, she still felt somewhat awkward alone with him.

Abruptly his mood changed again. "Of course this is pure selfishness on my part," he told her sadly.

She stared at him in bewilderment. "Why do you say that?"

"Because it is the truth," he went on with a surprising intensity. "From the moment of our first meeting I've been attracted by you. And yet I know I have no right."

"I don't feel that way," she said. "I see no reason why we shouldn't become good friends. Especially since we have a mutual interest in music and are going to be living here in the same house."

Ernest's expression was grim. "I warn you Elizabeth and the others may not feel the same way."

Victoria recalled the warnings the others had given her and knew he was right. But suddenly the warnings seemed unimportant. She liked Ernest Collins and she trusted him. She could not picture this gentle musician as a possible murderer.

"I say it is something for us to decide," she told him quietly.

He studied her silently, his handsome face now shadowed with the torment of his thoughts. "You must have heard something about my history." His voice was almost harsh.

"I know you've been desperately unhappy," she murmured. "I'm sorry you had to lose Elaine. You loved her so much!"

His eyes binned into her and he nodded. "Yes, I did love her. Loved her more than any human has a right to love another. With the accident my life ended. Since then I've merely endured."

She shook her head, afraid of this new mood of his, "Surely such a love shouldn't leave you so desolate. You were lucky to have had such a perfect relationship even for a little."

He listened to her with a strange expression. Then at last he said, "Yes. Yes, that could be one way of looking at it." But his voice was strained and lacked sincerity.

"You must learn to live with your sorrow and somehow find new things to interest you," she said. "A new life to enjoy. There is no perfection for any of us. I have lived all these years without knowing who my parents are."

"I'd almost forgotten about that," he said, turning away.

After a moment he went on, "Since you know about Elaine, you must also have heard about what happened here last summer."

It was a difficult moment. "Yes, I have. The girl who fell from the cliff."

He swung around to her, agony in his handsome face. "I was truly fond of Stella. I thought I might be in love with her. Then when it happened they began to ask questions. I knew what they were hinting—that I wasn't quite sane, that I had killed her. Because I suffered a nervous collapse once, they decided I had to be a murderer."

"That's because they don't really understand you," she said softly, a hand on his arm to comfort him.

His eyes met hers. "Are you sure you do? Can you be so certain that Stella wasn't murdered? That I wasn't the guilty one? Or at least shared the guilt?"

Victoria met his tortured gaze soberly. "I can't say whether or not she met her death accidentally," she told him. "But I am willing to stand on my belief that it was no fault of yours."

"Thank you!" he said. "Thank you, Victoria Winters!" The words seemed to choke him. Swiftly he grasped her arms and drew her close to him. His firm lips pressed tightly to hers, preventing any protest on her part and she knew there would have been no remonstrance from her in any case. She was completely fulfilled and happy in his embrace and she questioned neither his motives nor her easy surrender.

The close angry cry of a seagull broke the magic happiness of the moment. Slowly he released her with a bemused expression on his lean, handsome features. She was standing so that she was facing Collins House and for a fleeting second had the feeling that they might have been seen by someone standing up in the captain's walk. A hasty glance up at it showed her there was no basis for her fears. It was empty.

"There is fear in your face," he said, still staring at her.

She forced herself to smile. "Not true fear," she said. "The gull's cry made me shiver. It's such a sad sound and it came so close." She didn't intend to tell him that for an instant she'd felt unseen eyes spying on them from the grim old mansion.

He gave a deep sigh, his hands at his side. "What a stupid, cruel thing for me to do. Especially since I do care for you, Victoria."

"There's nothing to reproach yourself for," she said. "I enjoyed the kiss."

"Believe me, there was nothing casual about it."

She smiled at him tenderly. "You made that clear enough without any explanation."

"We'd better get back to the house," he said. "As it is, they'll probably be wondering what we're up to."

"I suppose so."

He took her by the arm and they started back. "There must be a way," he said quietly as they walked. "A way for us in which no one need be hurt." He gave her a loving glance. "Give me a week to think it over," he said. "By the time I come back I'll have made some decisions."

She gave him the tolerant smile she had so often bestowed on the children in the foundling home. For at this moment he seemed more an unhappy child than anything else. "There is no rush," she said. "We have plenty of time. We are still almost strangers."

He pressed her hand warmly. "Don't say that," he murmured. "We have never been strangers."

"One of my reasons for coming here," she went on, "was to find the truth about myself. I have reason to believe that is still possible. I think Elizabeth could help me if she would."

"Don't count too much on Elizabeth," Ernest warned her bitterly. "She is as twisted as the rest of us." They had come to the foot of the entrance steps and he paused before they went up them and into the house. He frowned. "I don't like the idea of going away and leaving you here."

"I'll be all right," she promised him. "I'll be busy with David's lessons. The days will pass quickly."

He made no reply because at that moment the great oak door swung open and Elizabeth Stoddard was frowning down at them.

"I've been wondering where you were," she told Victoria. "I have sent David to the library to wait your arrival and begin his lessons."

"I didn't know you intended me to start with him today," she apologized to the older woman.

"It seems better to begin at once," Elizabeth said crisply. "It will help keep him out of mischief!" There was a suggestion in her sharp tone that this would also be true in Victoria's case.

Ernest Collins was not unaware of his cousin's angry mood. He glanced at Victoria and advised, "You'd better hurry on in. If I'm any judge of David, he won't wait for you long."

She nodded. "You're right, of course!" She quickly mounted the steps and hurried past the indignant Elizabeth and on down the shadowed hallway to the library.

David was still there when she entered, standing disconsolately by an ancient globe of the world that was mounted on a stand by the window. He was regarding it with disdain as it whirled giddily. As Victoria came close to him he reached out and gave it an extra spin.

She laughed. "Come now! The world doesn't go around that fast! You'll have it off the stand and rolling across the carpet if you keep on."

He didn't look up. Continuing to frown at the dizzily spinning globe, he said, "It's out of date anyway! Miss Gordon said the boundaries are thirty years old and all wrong!"

Victoria sat down at the desk. "We still don't want it rolling over the floor, do we?"

David paid no attention to her, but stood watching the globe for a few minutes longer until it had come to a full stop. By that time she had set out a few sums for him to do and was ready to begin some arithmetic instruction.

The boy came to stand sullenly across from her. "Are you a friend of my father's?" he wanted to know.

"I've only just met him," she said.

"All the teachers who have come here before have been friends of my father's," David went on, "and I didn't like any of them."

"Not even Miss Gordon?"

"Miss Gordon was a creep!"

"Well, that's not a very nice word, David," she reproved him. He smiled nastily. "She wasn't a very nice person."

The youngster's adult manner and habit of talking back was not easy to cope with. She covered up her chagrin by concentrating on the lesson she had prepared for him.

He studied the page of the lesson book with the sums she had put down and said, "They're a cinch! I can do them easy!"

"Well, show me!" Victoria challenged him.

"Okay!" he said disgustedly and grasping the notebook huddled into one of the easy chairs and began to work at the sums at a furious pace.

Victoria watched him with an amused expression. There was something likable about the lad in spite of his difficult disposition. She could see that he was trying to impress her with the speed and ease with which he could do the sums. As she waited for the results she suddenly heard the distant sound of a violin and knew that Ernest Collins had begun his practice session upstairs. The music came in a masterly and thrilling manner to remind her that only a short time ago the young concert violinist had held her in his arms. The song of the violin became sweetly sad and she reviewed the romantic interlude between them and marveled that it had come about.

What would happen now? Ernest had seemed very serious in his declaration of love for her and she knew that she liked him a great deal. But she was aware of the barriers that might yet separate them. The young violinist was plainly still haunted by the tragic loss of his beloved Elaine and by the violent death of the other girl, Stella, last summer. She had the impression he had guilt feelings concerning the young artist's violent end and was certain there were facts surrounding the tragic event of which she was still unaware.

"There!" David Collins said proudly, passing her the book with the problems completed. "I told you I could do them in a few minutes."

"So you did!" she agreed, recalling herself to the present and quickly scanning the answers he had put down. She looked up again and smiled. "You've done very well. There is only one mistake."

He let out a howl of protest. "I didn't make any mistakes!"

"I'm afraid so," she said and held the book out for him to study it himself. "See?"

David scowled at the sum and reluctantly agreed that he had been out one decimal point. Then he tossed it aside. "I'm tired," he said. "I don't feel like doing lessons today."

"People have to learn to work, even if they don't feel like it," she warned him. "We can't make an exception for you. I have some history questions for you to answer next." She gave him another notebook with a half-dozen history items to be answered.

While he was busy with these she set about preparing a geography test. The violin music from upstairs had ended so there was nothing to distract her as she applied herself to her task. All at once she realized something was happening and she glanced up with dismay to see David hurrying to the door.

"David! Come back!" she shouted after him.

He made no reply. She rose quickly to follow him to the hall in time to see him race down the long corridor to the rear and vanish through a door to the left. Without hesitating she went after him. She found herself at the entrance to a steep flight of stairs that led to the cellar.

Knowing that she must assert her position at once or have the boy play pranks on her continually, she hurried down the stairs after him. The light was poor and the same damp staleness assailed her nostrils that she'd encountered when trying to enter the deserted east wing. But she was in no mood to be held back by an unpleasant smell. Her feet at last touched the hard earth of the cellar floor and she heard the boy's running footsteps far ahead.

There was a tunnel-like passage leading to the left, partially lighted by narrow basement windows at long intervals. Along its shadowed length young David had fled. She now followed him, realizing he had put her in a ridiculous position and knowing she was suffering a loss of dignity in her pursuit. But she could balance all that if she caught up with him and chastised him at once. There had to be an understanding between them.

Reaching the end of the passage, she found herself in a fairly large storage room that looked as if no one had entered it for years. As she went in, a thick, filthy cobweb caught in her hair and streaked down her cheek. She flipped it off with a grimace of revulsion.

"Where are you, David?" she called. "I know you have to be in here somewhere and I mean to get you and take you back upstairs."

Her voice echoed hollowly in the big dark room. She thought she heard a rustle in a far corner and her eyes darted toward where the sound had come from, but there was no sign of the fugitive. The room was piled high with old furniture, ancient bedsteads of iron, a double stack of books covered with dust, abandoned paintings stacked against each other, all the debris of years of existence in the old mansion. Again she thought she heard a sound, as if the hiding boy had suddenly changed position. She wheeled around to stare at a battered stand, sure that he must be crouching behind it.

"David, I order you to come out!" she said sternly.

When he did not reply she began to have her first doubts. Was it possible the youngster had eluded her? Perhaps there had been some turning that she had missed in her haste. David could have slipped back upstairs. The more she considered this the more likely it seemed.

She stood in the midst of the decay and dust and peered around her in the uncertain light that came from the shadowed passage since there seemed to be no windows in the room at all.

"David!" she called. This time her voice was weaker with a hint of her nervousness evident in it.

Again there was nothing but silence. Now she was sure the boy had tricked her. There was no point in her hesitating in this gloomy spot any longer. He had really made her look idiotic.

As she turned to start back to the passageway, the door was flung shut with a creaking of hinges and a mighty thud—she was a captive in the darkness of the storage room. It couldn't have been any errant wind that caught the door and swung it shut, she thought. David must have been hidden near the door and made a dash for it and closed it after him.

"David, come back!" she cried plaintively and began groping her way across the silent blackness of the room in the direction where she thought the door must be. But she had only gone a few steps when she tripped over something and fell forward with a panic-stricken cry.

Luckily she suffered no more damage than a scraped ankle and a stinging wrist that could indicate a sprain. She'd fallen with her full weight on that hand in an effort to protect herself. Cautiously she rose to her feet and advanced slowly again. It seemed an endless time before she finally reached the wall and began to search for the door. But her groping hands were unable to find it.

No longer could she put up a pretense of courage. Completely shaken, she sobbed out, "David! If you hear me, let me out! Please!"

She paused to listen but what she heard sent a fresh chill of terror through her crouched body. The sound came from the other side of the room and it was horribly familiar! It was the same soft scraping that had conjured up a terrifying vision of incredibly long fingernails tipping thin, misshapen hands and pawing blindly for a path to freedom. As before, this sound was followed by shuffling footsteps and heavy breathing. This thing from the darkness was coming nearer to her each moment!

"No!" she screamed, not knowing what she was protesting. "No!"

Something hit the base of her skull and she pitched forward into a canyon of night. Her fears and frantic thoughts ceased in that brief second.

It was Elizabeth's voice she heard first, anxious and insistent. "Can you hear me, Victoria? Open your eyes if you hear me!"

The words filtered slowly into her dulled brain. But the urgency with which they were uttered caused them to register in a muddled way. She knew the mistress of Collins House was demanding some sort of cooperation from her. She had no clear idea of what she was expected to do. She couldn't seem to organize her thoughts and her head ached wretchedly. With a supreme effort she opened her eyes; all was a blur for a moment. Then the haze cleared and she saw the alarmed face of Elizabeth with the others crowding behind her.

"Thanks Heavens!" Elizabeth said. "It seemed you would never come to."

Victoria slowly moved her head on the pillow and saw that she had been brought upstairs to her own room. She tried to think, vainly attempted to recall anything that had happened after that terrible moment of panic in the darkness, but it was all a blank to her.

"Don't crowd her, Mother," Carolyn protested.

"She'll be all right now," Elizabeth said with a touch of acerbity. "You do feel better, don't you?" she asked Victoria.

"Yes," she said weakly.

Ernest stood at the foot of her bed, looking angry. "I still say we should call a doctor!"

"It would certainly do no harm," Roger Collins chimed in. He was standing close to Carolyn.

"I doubt if that will be necessary," Elizabeth said stubbornly. Turning to Victoria she said, "I found you stretched out unconscious in the storage room under the east wing. We looked everywhere else for you and David said you had followed him downstairs."

"Yes," she said, her voice a little stronger. "I lost him and the door shut."

"He's admitted leading you into storage room," Elizabeth said grimly. "He says he didn't mean for you to get hurt and he's sorry."

Victoria was gradually regaining her senses. She looked up tensely at the older woman. "Someone came after me in the darkness. Struck me a blow!"

The attractive older woman stared down at her incredulously. "You must be imagining that. It's perfectly clear what happened. You stumbled in the darkness and fell."

"No!" Victoria raised herself slightly on an elbow. "Someone came after me. The same as in this room the other night."

Elizabeth gave Ernest an odd look. "What do you make of that?" she asked.

The handsome violinist looked pale and shaken. "I don't know," he said in a faltering tone. "Victoria, are you certain that you didn't merely panic and fall?"

"No," she said. "Someone struck me from behind." Elizabeth's face became grim. "If your story is true, then David has been lying again. He claims he was never in the storage room. But it's possible he was hiding there and came up on you in the darkness and struck you a coward's blow!"

"In which case he'll answer to me!" Roger Collins exploded angrily. "Son or no son, he'll not get away with such actions!" Victoria was startled. She had not meant to accuse David; she didn't believe he had attacked her. And she had no intention of seeing him blamed for something he hadn't done. The boy was in trouble enough as it was. She saw that she had no course but to protect him.

"Perhaps you're right," she told Elizabeth in a dull voice. "I probably did imagine it all. I know David wasn't in the room. Likely I struck my head when I stumbled." It was a lie, and she knew it and she had an idea Elizabeth knew it as well.

The older woman was quick to take her cue. "I'm glad it's cleared up in your mind," she said.

CHAPTER 6

Victoria sank back on her pillow and closed her eyes. Her head still throbbed wickedly and she felt completely exhausted. David had tricked her successfully; someone had knocked her out, and it was the final defeat that she must subscribe to their theory that she had received her head injury in a fall, in order to protect David.

Now Elizabeth spoke sharply to the others. "I think the room should be emptied. She needs rest and quiet. We can do her no good, crowding around her this way."

There were murmurs of reluctant agreement from the group and she heard them file out of her room. Then Elizabeth spoke to her again. "I'll send Carolyn in to keep you company later. Perhaps we should bring a cot in here and have her spend the night close to you."

Victoria opened her eyes and saw the older woman was bending over her anxiously. She was too confused to offer any suggestions. "Whatever you think best."

"Then we'll decide later," Elizabeth promised. "I am glad you're better and of course we're all distressed that such an unfortunate thing should happen so soon after your coming to join us."

"It was my own fault," she murmured.

The lovely face of the older woman was grave. "Do keep away from the east wing," she cautioned. "I'm sure I warned you once before that it is in a bad state of repair and not safe. What happened this afternoon is certainly proof of that."

"I'll remember," she said, as she shut her eyes once more. She heard Elizabeth leave the room and close the door after her. Then there was the sound of her footsteps retreating down the stairs. The room took on a ghostly silence. There was only the distant wash of the waves against the shore to intrude on the hushed stillness. Victoria opened her eyes and frowned. Now she knew she was actually in danger as long as she remained in the old mansion. Yet there was no possibility of leaving Collins House until she had found answers to some questions of long standing.

While she had lied to save David from being accused of attacking her, she had not swayed from her original conviction that she had been struck down by someone else. Somebody in the rambling old house wanted to kill her! The person had made a full-fledged attempt in the storage room and it was only good luck the blow had turned out to be a glancing one and she had escaped its full force. Otherwise she would have died there in the darkness and Elizabeth would have been just as quick to assume it was an accident as she had been a few minutes ago.

It seemed to Victoria the mistress of Collins House had been entirely too eager to put her injuries down to a fall. It was as if she knew who was guilty and was determined to shield him—or her. There had to be a motive for attempted murder; it occurred to Victoria that the motive in her case might be to prevent her from discovering her identity. Someone in Collins House knew the truth of her origins and could not let her stumble onto the secret.

She could think of no other reason for the attack. She began to wonder if Elizabeth herself might have a hand in the crime. If she needed a confederate there was no question that she could count on the loyalty of Matt Morgan. Perhaps he had been the one who had struck her down. Yet she had the feeling that it had been a smaller person who had shuffled toward her in the darkness. It had all happened so quickly she would never be able to decide surely.

Ernest had looked shaken and angry. Roger Collins had seemed more upset by what had taken place than Victoria would have expected. Even Carolyn seemed to have temporarily lost her high spirits. Perhaps more than one of them knew why an attempt had been made on her life.

Her thoughts were suddenly interrupted by a sound in the corridor outside her door. As she raised herself on an elbow, she was startled to see the handle of the door turn gently. Then the door itself opened very gradually. Stifling a scream, she waited for a hint of who it might be.

When David's small figure was revealed a moment later she

was glad she hadn't made any outcry. He stood with his hand on the knob, looking frightened, and then edged across the room to the foot of her bed.

"I've come to ask your pardon," he said shamefacedly. "Did Elizabeth or your father send you?"

He shook his head. "No. They told me not to bother you. It's my own idea."

At once Victoria warmed to the frank youngster "I don't blame you for what happened, David," she said, "although it was wrong for you to lead me on such a chase."

He stared down at the carpet. "I know. I won't do it again."

"I hope you'll remember that," she said.

The boy raised his eyes and with a burst of enthusiasm promised, "And I'll work hard at my lessons, too! I promise." Victoria smiled. Perhaps there would be at least one dividend as a result of her terrifying experience. From now on David might be on her side.

"We'll see how you carry out your good intentions tomorrow," she said.

"I mean it. You'll see!" David smiled in return. "Good-bye, Miss Winters." He hurried off.

The boy's visit was a heartening experience after the ordeal of the day. She lay back feeling satisfied and dropped off into a light sleep for a short while. When she awoke it was dinner time and Carolyn arrived with a tray of food for her.

Victoria sat up in bed. "I think I could have gone down for dinner," she said. "I do feel a lot better."

The teenager put the tray on the bedside table. "You'll rest in bed until tomorrow, at least," she insisted. "Mother says you must. Whether you know it or not, there's a half-inch cut in your scalp where you hit it."

She raised a hand gingerly to the injured spot. "I know it." Carolyn sighed. "Just my luck! I had it all planned for us to drive in to the Blue Whale tonight! Joe will be there waiting for me and he'll wonder what's happened."

"I'm afraid there'll be no frugging for me tonight," Victoria told her with a faint smile.

"Well, another night," Carolyn said. "I've brought you up some toast and soup and a bit of pudding. If you want anything else, just ask for it."

She glanced at the tray. "I don't know whether I can manage even that. I'm still a bit nauseated."

"You must try! And later we're bringing in a cot and I'm going to stay in here tonight and until your nerves are settled."

"That's not fair," Victoria protested. "You shouldn't have to leave your good bed and room because of me. I'll be all right." "I want to come," Carolyn said with a delighted smile. "It will be fun. A real change for me! We can talk until all hours!"

"Not unless my head stops aching."

"I mean when you're feeling better," Carolyn added quickly. Carolyn obviously enjoyed the novelty of playing nurse. She hovered over Victoria, offering advice, food, and service all the while Victoria ate. When the girl finally left with the tray of dirty dishes, she was thankful to be alone. She knew she shouldn't be annoyed, since Carolyn, like David, was desperately lonely, yet she was overdoing her role of nurse. And the prospect of having her sleeping in the room was to be regarded as a mixed blessing at best.

Victoria felt better after having eaten and again enjoyed a period of quiet and rest. Dusk was settling and the room was filled with the murky grayness of early evening when a soft knocking came on her door.

She quickly sat up, drawing the coverings to her. Her voice sounded thin as she asked, "Yes? Who is it?"

From the other side of the door a familiar voice said, "It's Ernest. May I come in a moment?"

With a sigh of relief she answered, "Yes. Please do!"

The door opened and he came in, hesitating by the door a moment. "You're sure you feel well enough to see me?"

"Of course. Sit down for a while."

He carefully closed the door after him and came across the room. He was carrying something that looked like a framed picture. He set this against the wall before taking the plain chair beside her bed.

Even in the blurred late twilight he made a handsome figure. He took her hand gently in his. "I have to leave first thing in the morning," he said. "That is why I wanted to come in now and say good-by."

"I'm glad you did."

"I'm going to worry about you more than ever."

"I'll be all right."

He tightened his grip on her hand. "After today I'm not so sure." He paused. "Are you certain you fell? You changed your story so quickly."

Even though she liked Ernest Collins and believed in him, she could not bring herself to be perfectly frank about the happenings in the underground storage room at this point.

After the slightest pause she murmured, "It was an accident. I fell and struck my head."

"There must be no more accidents," he said in a tight voice.

"I know how you feel. I promise to be especially careful."

He bent urgently toward her. "Don't trust anyone in this

house, Victoria. Do you hear that? Don't trust any of them!"

"Very well," she said, startled at his intensity.

"I can't explain now, but I have a good reason for saying that. I want to come back next week and find you here and well."

"I will be," she said, trying to strike a cheerful note. "David has promised to be a model student and that's surely a step in the right direction."

"Be careful of him as well. He can be a little monster when he likes. And don't forget he was the decoy who led you into danger today."

A glance at his face told her that Ernest was not joking. "I hadn't thought of him as a decoy," she admitted. "I took it for granted that he just decided to play a prank on me and did."

"There is that other possibility," the violinist pointed out grimly.

She glanced at the spot where he'd put the item he'd brought into the room. "You have something with you. What is it?"

"I'll show you," he said, standing up in the growing darkness. "We'll need some light."

"There's only the bed lamp," she said, switching it on. Ernest picked up the fairly large painting and brought it to the bedside for her inspection. "I thought you'd be interested in seeing this."

It was a colorful study of the lawns, the cliffs and the sea beyond. The perspective indicated that it had been done from some high point in Collins House. Glancing up at Ernest, she said, "It's very good. Was it done from the roof?"

He nodded. "The captain's walk. It's an example of Stella's work. One of the last things she ever did."

She was a little taken back but pretended to be engrossed in the painting. "She must have had a lot of talent," she said. "Stella was unusually gifted." There was deep unhappiness in his tone. "I've had this in my room. I've decided to dispose of it. I thought you might like it."

"Of course," she said. "I'm sure I can find a place for it."

"She gave it to me," he said, his burning eyes fixed on her. "Now I'm passing it on to you."

Before Victoria realized it, she had blurted out, "Stella had an accident, too."

Ernest Collins did not flinch but nodded slowly. "Yes," he agreed. "She had an accident, too. A fatal one."

Victoria was blushing. She touched a hand to her temple. "I don't know what made me say that! I'm still a little addled."

"No reason why you shouldn't be," he said, his eyes still on her. "You had a nasty blow. It could easily have killed you." He took the painting over and placed it on a chair. Then he came back to her bedside. "I won't stay any longer. Remember what I told you."

"I will."

He bent close and touched his lips lightly to hers. "We'll have plenty to talk over when I return," he said with a small smile. He continued to study her a moment with sad eyes as if loath to leave. Then he stood up straight, nodded brusquely, and left the room.

Victoria felt strange about his visit. It was to be expected that he would come in to say good-by before he left. But something in his manner had made him more of an enigma than ever before. Why had he chosen this time to leave the painting by the dead Stella with her?

She remembered his odd behavior when they had seen that phantom figure staring down at them as they stood together on the spot where Stella had met her death. Elizabeth had said she thought Ernest had seen her standing on the captain's walk and thought her Stella's ghost.

Now the painting of the cliffs was here in the room with her— the view as seen through the dead girl's eyes and fixed on the canvas for all time. Was there some secret revealed in Stella's vision of the cliff that Ernest Collins now wanted her to see? Victoria let her gaze rest on the painting in the chair for a moment and was startled to discover she was trembling.

It was a relief when Carolyn arrived with Matt Morgan, who carried a cot which he set up. As they were getting ready for bed, Carolyn discovered the painting and asked, "Where did you get this?"

"Ernest made me a present of it."

Carolyn raised her eyebrows. "Generous Ernest! I wonder why? You know who painted this, of course?"

"Stella."

"Stella," the teenager agreed. "I didn't know there were any of her things around. Her parents came to the cottage and took all her belongings."

"This was a personal gift to Ernest before her death," she said. "He's had it in his room until now."

Carolyn gave her attention to the painting again. "Poor Cousin Ernest! First Elaine and then Stella! It's gruesome when you think about it, but falling in love with him could be dangerous." She glanced over at Victoria. "I wouldn't care to be his third dead love!"

She managed a wan smile. "Aren't you being a little melodramatic?"

Carolyn laughed. "Just plain kookie, darling! And not much wonder!" She went over to the wall where the painting of the clipper ship hung. "I'm tired of this anyway," she said. "Let's give it a rest and hang Stella's masterpiece." She quickly removed the clipper ship and hung the view of the cliff in its place. Then she stepped back and studied it. "I think it's an improvement, don't you?"

"It's a nice painting," Victoria agreed. "I haven't examined it closely and I'm afraid I'm too tired to do it tonight."

"A hint!" Carolyn laughed. "I won't keep you awake any longer. I'll put this old painting in the closet and then you can turn off the light."

A few minutes later Carolyn settled down on the cot and Victoria snapped off the bed lamp. With the room in darkness and the knowledge that Carolyn was only a few feet away, she allowed the weariness that had been gradually engulfing her to take full possession. Yet some of the things Ernest had said were still troubling her. He had warned her not to trust anyone in Collins House. Not anyone.

Surely he couldn't be including Carolyn in that warning. Carolyn, who occupied the cot so close to her and on whom she was depending for company during the long hours of darkness ahead. But he had said not to trust anyone. It was a disquieting thought, especially when she was so far gone in sleep she could not force herself to come awake and cope with it. With this final concession to her exhausted state, she dozed off.

And even though she awoke to a morning of fog and a light drizzle of rain, she felt refreshed and much happier. Carolyn had gotten up before she was awake and now returned with a breakfast tray.

Victoria sat up in bed. "You're spoiling me," she protested. "I'm well enough to go down and get my own breakfast."

"We'll see about that," Carolyn said, arranging the tray for her. "Meanwhile, I've brought up everything you like." She moved across to the window. "It's a rotten day. I wonder if Cousin Ernest's plane took off from Bangor."

"I hope so," she said, picking up a glass of orange juice. "He might miss the first of his concerts otherwise."

Carolyn turned to her. "He left really early. Just after dawn. Of course, it's a fifty mile drive to Bangor from here."

"I know," she said, suddenly interested. "Have you been up there often?"

The other girl shook her head. "We do most of our shopping in Ellsworth or drive on to Boston. By 'we,' I mean Uncle Roger and me. It's been years since Mother's gone anywhere."

"But of course she has you and Roger do errands for her."

"Naturally." Carolyn was wearing blue jeans and a white cardigan with a gay little robin embroidered on the pocket. She leaned on the arm of the easy chair by the casement window.

"Has Roger made regular trips to Bangor?" Victoria asked, still thinking about those payments that had come to her at the foundling home every month until she was sixteen in an envelope bearing a Bangor postmark.

"More or less," she said with a shrug. "He always heads straight for the nearest liquor store. And if Ellsworth is closed, that's bound to be Bangor."

"I see," Victoria said. It seemed she wasn't to get any information from Carolyn. But then, the girl would have been too young to have taken any notice of special mailings from Bangor.

Carolyn suddenly stood up. "I'd forgotten," she said. "It seems such a long while ago. But I used to go to Bangor at least once a week with Matt Morgan. We had a lot of chickens here for a while until the building burned down. Matt used to take the eggs directly to a wholesale house in Bangor every week and I drove up there with him on the truck."

Victoria's interest was caught. "When did he stop going?"

The other girl considered. "It must be about four years," she said. "Yes. It was exactly four years ago."

Four years ago! Victoria found herself becoming excited. That would be when she was sixteen! And the payments from Bangor had ended exactly at that time! Of course, it could all be coincidence, but she wondered. Had Elizabeth used Matt to mail those monthly letters to the foundling home? It was another of the questions to which she must find an answer.

Carolyn's mother arrived just as Victoria was finishing her coffee. She assured the older woman that she was feeling much better and would be down shortly to work with David.

Elizabeth appraised her skeptically. "You still don't look too well."

"I'm perfectly all right," Victoria protested.

The older woman gave a slight shrug. "Do as you like, then." As she turned to go, she saw Stella's painting of the cliff. She stared at it for a moment. "Where did that come from?"

"Your cousin brought it in here last night," she said. "He thought I'd be interested in seeing it."

Elizabeth's attractive face wore a veiled expression as she gazed at Victoria over her shoulder. "Really? How clever of him." With a final glance at the painting she left.

Again Victoria found herself puzzled. Why should the older woman refer to Ernest's gesture as clever? Was there something about this business of the painting that had so far escaped her?

When she had dressed she went over and studied the picture in detail. It was an excellent painting but barren of anything to excite her curiosity. She searched in vain for even a tiny item to give her a clue as to any secrets it might hold.

David had come in from a run outdoors and was waiting for

her in the foyer. Together they went into the library and he proved as good as his word. He worked so quickly and well that they finished their morning quota well before noon and he was left with the better part of an hour to play. Victoria spent a quarter-hour preparing the afternoon's lessons and then went out to the foyer again.

Roger Collins appeared in the doorway of the drawing room with his usual brandy glass in hand. "On a damp day like this a brandy does wonders for the appetite," he told her.

She paused in the hallway, facing him. "I had no idea the weather had a bearing on it."

"It works on a dry, sunshiny day as well," he added with a wink. "The all-year-round remedy." He drained his glass.

"I usually find a walk helps me enjoy luncheon," she said. "But it's too wet out now to think about it."

Roger eyed her with some interest. "You've made a remarkably quick recovery from your happening."

"I was lucky to escape as easily as I did," she said.

He nodded. "So it seems. I didn't want to press you last night, but I hope you'll forgive me a question or two now. Why did you change your story of what happened down there?"

She tried to bluff. "I don't know that I did."

"Come now, Victoria," he said with another wink. "I'm a veteran liar myself. President of the local Liars' Club, as a matter of fact. Don't try to put me off that way."

Victoria bit her lip. "I was confused. It took me a few minutes to remember clearly."

He shook his head. "That won't do either. Elizabeth put the words in your mouth and you repeated them. Before that you had said very plainly that someone had struck you in the darkness."

"I was wrong."

"I wonder." He paused. "I hope you haven't gone to all this trouble merely to protect David."

"Of course not," she protested.

His eyes held a cruel gleam. "Because if that's it. I'll find out sooner or later and thrash him within an inch of his life!"

"Don't you harm that boy!" she said hotly. "You've injured him enough as it is."

A thin smile played about Roger's mouth. "You're especially attractive when you're angry, Victoria. I suppose it is perverse of me to notice."

Carolyn came down the stairs to join them. Noticing her uncle's empty glass, she rolled her eyes and said, "Isn't it time for a refill, Roger darling?"

He chuckled. "Thanks for bringing it to my attention." He turned and went back into the drawing room.

Carolyn moved close to her and whispered conspiratorially, "I'm planning to go into the village tonight. Don't let me down. You'll be well enough to come along."

"Your mother is bound to object," Victoria protested. "And anyway, I can't promise how I'll feel by evening."

"I'll talk Mother into it this afternoon," the other girl said. "I don't want to miss getting in town tonight. There's bound to be a big gang at the Blue Whale. None of the boys go out fishing when it's foggy like this."

"We'll see," Victoria said, wanting to put her off easily. "And I have a good excuse for your coming along," she said. "You drive, don't you?"

"A little," she admitted. "I have a license."

"Great!" Carolyn exulted. "I want you to drive my car into Collinsport and leave it at the garage for a change of oil and some motor work. I'll drive the truck and go ahead of you and we can both come back in it."

Victoria frowned. "I'm not sure I want to drive on a foggy night on a road I don't know. And your car will be strange to me."

"It's nothing exotic! Just a plain six-cylinder convertible, four years old," she said. "I've only been driving two years on a special license."

"We'll talk about it later," Victoria said, hoping Carolyn would forget the excursion during the day. But it didn't work out that way.

She had just finished David's afternoon lessons and dismissed the boy when Elizabeth approached her in the library. "Carolyn tells me you have offered to drive her car into the village tonight," she said. "Are you certain you're well enough?"

Not wanting to let the other girl down, she said, "I think so." Carolyn's mother looked a little less than pleased. "She seems determined that you should go. I'll depend on you to see that she doesn't stay out too late."

"Yes, Mrs. Stoddard," Victoria said.

"And you'd better go out to the garage and get a little familiar with her car before you attempt to drive it."

Victoria decided to follow her advice. Slipping on her trench coat, she went out by the back door and headed toward the bam that had long ago been converted into a garage. The door was open and as she came close to it Roger Collins appeared from inside. He seemed somewhat disconcerted to see her.

"Seen anything of Matt Morgan?" he wanted to know as she came up to him.

"No," she said. "I expected to find him here."

"He's never around when you want him," Roger grumbled and went back toward the house.

She wondered at his somewhat furtive behavior and his hurry to get away, instead of lingering around attempting to paw her as he usually did. She found Carolyn's car parked beside the truck and saw that it had regular steering and automatic transmission. Satisfied that it would present no problem, she, too, returned to the house without seeing Morgan.

The hours passed quickly and Carolyn grew more excited as the time drew near for them to leave. She was on edge until they left for the garage and picked up the cars as planned. Morgan was around now to glare at Victoria as she backed Carolyn's convertible out into the foggy darkness.

Carolyn, who already had the truck in the yard, jumped out to come over and tell her, "Keep close behind me and mind the bumps. It's plenty rough!"

"I'll do my best," Victoria promised grimly, wondering why she had let herself in for this adventure. Carolyn drove the truck toward the road and she followed.

It was rough all the way. The taillights of the truck bounced ahead in the darkness; Victoria gritted her teeth and held tightly to the wheel of the convertible. They were starting down one of the long, steep grades in the narrow road when Victoria first noticed the extreme looseness of the wheel. Terrified, she realized she no longer had control of the steering. The car gained momentum.

CHAPTER 7

Victoria made a last frantic attempt to get some response from the steering wheel, which swung uselessly in her hands. With horror she felt the speeding car swerve from the narrow road and head straight down toward a giant boulder on the right side. She jammed down on the brake pedal as hard as she could and at the same time reached for the emergency brake handle and dragged it back.

The light car swerved even more madly and seemed about to turn upside down as the brakes locked and the tires squealed. And still its wild runaway pace was only partly checked. Victoria closed her eyes as the giant boulder loomed closer under the glow of her headlights. And then the crashing impact came. Victoria was thrown against the wheel as the car struck and then lurched far over on one side.

She was still in the car when Carolyn came running back up the road screaming her name. It took their combined efforts to get the door open on her side and then, her head still reeling, she clumsily got out and leaned weakly against the wrecked vehicle.

Carolyn was almost in tears. "Victoria, are you all right? You're not hurt, are you?"

She at last recovered enough from her shock to say, "I was lucky. The brakes slowed it enough to cut down the force of the impact." Her voice was thin and she was trembling.

The other girl put an arm around her. "I couldn't imagine what had happened when I looked in the rear-view mirror and saw your lights swing away from the road."

Victoria said, "The steering. Something went wrong. The wheel turned and I had no control."

"I heard the crash as I got out of the truck. I was sure you'd be killed!"

Carolyn's words were harmless enough, natural, even, under the circumstances, but there was a certain inflection in her voice that struck Victoria as odd. She gave the teen-ager a quick glance and wondered if the accident had come as such a surprise to her.

She said, "Have you ever had any trouble with the steering before?"

Carolyn shook her head. "No. I've been hearing this odd noise from the motor and that's why I planned to leave it in the village for work." She gave a despairing glance at the wreckage. "I guess now I'll only need the tow truck to take it to the dump."

Victoria was gradually recovering from her shock and now she turned and surveyed the damaged car herself. "It may not be as bad as you think," she said. "I'm sorry. I did all I could to avoid the accident."

"I'm sure you did," the other girl agreed quickly. "Don't think anything about it. Uncle Roger made me buy collision insurance. I'm glad now. It will help me get another car. That is, if Mother will allow me to have one after this."

"Hadn't we better go back to the house?"

Carolyn said, "No. Anyway, I'll have to notify the garage to come and get this in the morning. After that we may as well go to the Blue Whale and have a little fun."

Victoria found herself still wary of the other girl. "I don't feel much like fun at this moment," she said.

"And I don't blame you. But by the time we've driven into the village I'm sure you'll feel better," Carolyn insisted. She leaned forward through the open car door and switched off the lights. "No need to leave them burning," she said.

She realized there was little point in arguing. Carolyn had apparently made up her mind to go on to the village no matter what. They walked ahead to the truck, not saying much. Nor did they do a lot of talking during the drive to the village. Victoria sat huddled in a corner of the truck cab, thinking about the accident.

She still had the uneasy feeling that Carolyn had known the accident would happen. She knew that this might not be fair, but she could not shake off the suspicion. There had been something just a little too pat in Carolyn's reaction to it all.

Yet all the others in the house knew that they were driving to the village and that Victoria would be taking Carolyn's car. It would have been easy for Elizabeth to instruct Matt Morgan to tamper with the car. He was a fair mechanic, according to Carolyn; he would know just what to do to weaken the steering.

And then she remembered her encounter with Roger in the garage doorway and how furtive he had seemed at that time. What had he been doing there? He'd said he was looking for Matt Morgan but this could be merely an alibi. Roger could have tampered with the car. But for what reason?

Again she was faced with the fact that if someone at Collins House wanted to kill her it must be because she presented a threat to them. It had to be something to do with her origin and the mysterious payments that had been sent her from Bangor.

Carolyn interrupted her troubled thoughts by bringing the truck to a jolting halt in front of the dingy service station with its single neon sign and saying, "Excuse me for just a minute, Victoria. I want to tell him about my car."

She waited while the other girl hurried into the garage and hastily conferred with a middle-aged man working on a car over the grease pit. After a few minutes Carolyn returned and they drove on to the Blue Whale, which was located a halfblock to the left of the main street. Outside, it looked like some ramshackle factory building with its ancient clapboards and peeling paint. Its only distinction was a small blue neon sign spelling its name.

Victoria followed Carolyn inside and flinched slightly at the noisy laughter in the place, the roaring jukebox and the stale smell of cigarette smoke and liquor. It was as crowded as the teen-ager had predicted. Almost all the stools at the bar were filled and most of the booths along the side as well. At the far end, near the gaudy neon rainbow of the jukebox, a few tables and chairs were set out. Four or five young couples were spiritedly doing some version of the twist on the tiny floor. Without question this was Collinsport's swinging center.

Carolyn was greeted on all sides as a popular regular of the place and a good-looking young man in dark trousers and a tight black turtleneck sweater slid easily off one of the bar stools and came over to her.

"Lover!" Carolyn said happily as she opened her arms to him.

"Hi!" The young man smiled lazily as he embraced her and planted a resounding kiss on her lips. Then he gave an inquiring grin Victoria's way. "Who's the new chick?"

"This is Victoria Winters," Carolyn said proudly. "She's living at the house now. I've been telling you about Joe, Victoria. Meet Joe Haskell!"

"Hello, Joe," Victoria said with as much enthusiasm as she could muster after her upsetting experience and in the face of all this confusion.

"Welcome to the jungle, Victoria," Joe said with another of his lazy smiles.

"Let's sit down, Joe," the teen-ager said. "I'm really shattered. And I mean shattered. We had an awful accident on the way here."

Joe looked only slightly interested as if he had heard stories of this sort from Carolyn before. He waved to an empty booth. "Take a seat," he told them. "I'll order us three beers." Victoria and Carolyn sat opposite each other in one of the plain wooden booths. Carolyn leaned forward with a proud smile. "How do you like it?"

She wanted to be polite. "It's about what I expected."

"Isn't Joe Haskell cute?"

"He seems very nice."

"A lot too young for me," Carolyn said, sitting back with a grown-up air and warning her with a nod that Joe was on his way back with the beers.

"Best draught beer in Maine," he promised Victoria as he sat the three big foam-topped glasses on the table. He took his place beside Carolyn and put an arm around her. "Now give out with the details of this shattering accident!" he ordered.

Carolyn was only too ready to go into a vivid account of the car going out of control and Victoria's almost miraculous escape from injury or death. Joe listened, plainly impressed, and from time to time made suitable shocked comments and turned to include Victoria in his reactions.

"Sounds like you're minus one convertible," he said at last and took a big gulp of his beer.

"I'll get another," Carolyn promised. "There's insurance and I can talk Mother into anything."

Joe grinned and winked for Victoria's benefit. "How about talking her into a son-in-law? Like me!"

"I could if I wanted to," Carolyn boasted. "The company has already given you a couple of promotions. And I guess you got them mainly because my mother mentioned you to the manager."

Joe frowned suddenly. "Now don't start that. If I really thought I didn't win those promotions on my own, I'd leave the company and get out of Collinsport pronto!"

"I was only joking," Carolyn said contritely.

The young man still seemed annoyed. "Sometimes I don't get your jokes. And that kind of talk isn't funny!"

Carolyn rolled her eyes and appealed to Victoria. "Just a stupid boy!" she said in her most sophisticated way.

The music from the jukebox blared on and many of the young people in the shabby place stopped at their table. Victoria found herself going through a ridiculous number of introductions to strangers of whose faces she instantly forgot and who looked equally uninterested in her. Joe went to the bar and brought back another round of beers for them and shortly afterward invited Carolyn to dance.

Victoria was left alone in the booth. She glanced down at her half-finished second beer and was filled with a desire to leave the noisy place and go back to Collins House. She was worried about Elizabeth's reaction to the accident and knew that in any case they shouldn't linger in the village too long. Her mind drifted to Ernest and she wondered where he might be at this moment. No doubt on the stage of a concert hall in some far away midwestern city. She decided she preferred the delicate classical music of his violin to the grunting sounds emanating from the jukebox. She felt lonely and miserable and began to wonder if her purpose in coming to Collinsport was doomed to failure.

She lifted her eyes to suddenly see a new and familiar figure at the bar—a tall, handsome man in a dark suit who was buying a package of cigarettes. It was Will Grant, the young lawyer she'd met the first night of her arrival in the area. Having completed his purchase, he turned, mechanically opening the cigarette package as he quickly scanned the place. The moment he saw her he came over.

"We meet in the most unexpected places," he said with a smile.

Victoria made no attempt to hide her pleasure in seeing him again. "I've been thinking of you," she said, "and wondering when I'd see you."

He glanced at the empty seat. "May I join you?" he asked.

"Yes. I'm here with Carolyn Stoddard and a friend."

"Oh," he said, glancing toward the dance floor. "I see her and Joe out there. I don't think they'll mind my stealing their seat for a few minutes." He sat across from her. "I don't often come in here, but I needed cigarettes. I'm glad I did." He studied her with a faint smile. "Had any more accidents?"

"As a matter of fact, I have," she said. She told him what had happened while he lit his cigarette and listened with quiet attention.

"That was really something tonight," he said when she'd finished. "You're lucky to be alive."

"I'm beginning to think so," she said.

His eyes fixed on her questioningly. "What do you think about Collins House and its people?"

She lowered her eyes to her glass. "That could be a long story."

"I have plenty of time."

At this point Carolyn and Joe Haskell returned and protested noisily when Will Grant stood up to give them their side of the booth. "No," Carolyn told him, pushing him back down onto the seat. "Joe and I want to visit around with some of the others anyway. That is, if you'll excuse us, Victoria." She smiled knowingly as if she was sure Victoria wouldn't object to being left in the young lawyer's company and moved along with Joe in tow.

When they were alone again Will Grant said, "I hope I haven't broken up your party."

"I was the unwanted third," she said with a laugh. "Or at least the third. I'm sure they're thankful they don't have to keep sitting here entertaining me."

"I'd consider that a pleasure," he said. "To resume. I'd like to hear something about you and why you decided to take this position with the Collins family."

Partly because she instinctively liked him and partly because she was aware he knew the Collins family intimately as their lawyer, she had no compunctions about going into detail about herself and her experiences at the old mansion. The noisy chatter on all sides and the loud rhythms of the jukebox assured them a kind of privacy and so she spoke freely.

He was a good listener. "Your personal problem interests me as a lawyer," he said. "If I can be of service in any way, don't hesitate to call on me. I go to Bangor a lot and have access to all the court records."

Victoria frowned thoughtfully. "It's just occurred to me that Augusta is the state capital and that's where all the vital statistics are kept. If my birth was recorded in this state, the records should be there."

"We'd want a few more details for a start," he said. "If you can provide them I'll get a friend of mine in Augusta to check the state records."

"I can't provide any details now," she said with a sigh. "I don't even know the exact date I was born. The authorities at the foundling home registered it tentatively as January I, 1946."

He smiled. "At least we know you're twenty."

"About twenty," she corrected him.

"One thing strikes me about your reception at Collins House," he said, stubbing out his cigarette in the tray between them. "Your friendship with Ernest Collins."

Because she knew she was blushing, Victoria was thankful for the Blue Whale's dim lighting. She had not divulged the full extent of her friendship with Ernest but had mentioned they'd had private talks and that he seemed the most understanding person in the grim mansion.

Now she suggested, "You have a special interest in Ernest Collins?"

"Because I know Ernest very well. We grew up together as boys here."

"You sound as if you don't like him," she said.

His bronzed face took on a guarded look. "I used to like him a lot."

"But not anymore?"

He hesitated. "Let's just say I'm not so sure about him these days."

"He is very talented."

"Granted," the young lawyer agreed.

"And he has had a tragic life."

"True again."

Victoria raised her eyebrows. "It seems to me you should sympathize with him, since you used to be his friend."

"I have every desire to be sympathetic toward Ernest," he was quick to assure her. "But there happen to be facts that I can't close my eyes to."

She stared at his solemn face and knew what he meant. He must have played an important part in the investigation of Stella's death last summer. And if anyone would have a thorough knowledge of the incident, he would.

She said, "You're thinking about that accident. What happened to Stella last summer."

His eyes met hers. "Was it an accident?"

She flinched a little. "Yes. I think so. Ernest says it was. I believe him."

"Ernest says it was," he repeated quietly. "But then, is Ernest really able to testify in the matter?"

Victoria stared at him. "I wish you'd come right out and say what you mean!"

He smiled grimly. "I will. And I warn you, the story goes back to Ernest's marriage."

She was immediately interested. "But, of course, you must have known Elaine! They lived here for several years. Was she as lovely as they say? I've never seen any pictures of her."

Will Grant nodded. "Elaine was one of the most beautiful women I've ever met. She was also extremely clever. And she was an excellent violinist, although not a genius like Ernest."

"Beautiful, clever and talented," Victoria said wistfully. "No wonder her death crushed him. No wonder he has eyes for no other woman."

"It should have made for a happy combination," Will Grant said. "Elaine had the three qualities that most people wish for and yet it all ended in tragedy."

"That dreadful accident," she said. "And he was miles away when it happened. It must have been awful for him."

"The waiting to discover whether she would live or die made it even more a torture for him," the lawyer said quietly. "I have only been able to gather a fragment of the story here and there. But I believe she lingered on for almost two weeks, although the doctors warned him she must die."

"And he waited all that time, hoping!"

"Probably that is why the scars went so deep with him," Will Grant admitted. "But from what I've been told it was fortunate that Elaine died. She'd suffered major head injuries and the lovely face of which she'd been so proud was shattered beyond even the hope of plastic surgery. Combined with the brain damage she must also have had, life could not have been bearable for her had she survived."

"How cruel!" Victoria said softly.

"Ernest behaved very strangely after her death. He just slipped out of sight and took on a hermit-like existence in a cottage he bought near Santa Barbara. He lived there alone for better than a year. Perhaps the rugged cliffs and the ocean reminded him of her and gave him some comfort. When he returned to Collinsport he was the nervous, haunted type he is now. I could hardly reach him when I tried to make general conversation. His main desire was to close his own house and live quietly with Elizabeth. She even opened up one of the shut-off apartments on the second floor to please him."

"He has a room in the main section of the house now."

"I know that," Will Grant said. "But he didn't make that change until after the business of Stella. When the investigation of her death was over he went away on a tour. It was on his return that he told Elizabeth he no longer wanted to occupy the apartment."

Victoria raised his eyebrows. "I wonder why?"

"Just another of the many mysteries about the man," the young lawyer said, looking down at the table top. "I was involved to quite an extent in the police inquiries into Stella's violent death."

"Had you known her?"

He nodded. "We were quite good friends. And when she told me of her interest in Ernest I warned her to be careful." His eyes met hers. "Just as I'm warning you now."

"I'm sure my case is quite different," she protested.

"Don't be too sure," he cautioned. "Stella seemed the ideal person to bring Ernest back to a normal life. I watched them together and could see him improve week by week. Even Elizabeth mentioned it to me."

"Then her accident must have been another dreadful blow to him."

"He gave every appearance that it was." Will Grant's rugged young face was shadowed. "And I wanted to believe him. Yet I can never forget that crumpled body on the rocks, nor the lack of evidence of what caused her fall."

"It was a foggy night, I understand," she said. "Couldn't she have ventured too near the edge of the cliff and slipped on the wet rock surface?"

"Stella knew the cliffs so well I find that hard to believe."

"Could she have been a suicide?"

"The police seemed to think that the most acceptable theory." He shrugged. "Though I can't see why, personally."

Victoria found herself resenting the young lawyer's implication that the only possible solution to the young artist's death was that Ernest had killed her. She said, "Must you blame Ernest? Is that the kind of friend you are?"

Will Grant looked at her with sad eyes. Nothing was said between them for a moment. The jukebox switched to a loud and monotonous new record that was almost exactly like the one that had just ended. The laughter and the noisy talk continued to blend with the tinkle of glasses and the regular ringing of the cash register.

At last he said, "Perhaps I should tell you this. But during the investigation it was discovered that Ernest had some trouble with the police during the year after Elaine's death when he lived in Santa Barbara."

Victoria was hit by a cold wave of apprehension. The tone of Will Grant's voice and the manner in which he weighed his words caused her to realize this was an important and perhaps a damning revelation she was about to hear.

She said, "Yes?"

"About six months after Elaine's death he began seeing a girl," Will said. " A lovely girl with an excellent social background. The friendship developed and it was accepted he would ask her to be his wife. Then, one night after they'd spent the evening together, the girl was attacked in the garden of her home. Someone cruelly lashed her across the face with a length of chain. She was so badly injured she required plastic surgery."

Victoria stared at him incredulously. "What could that have to do with Ernest?"

"They weren't able to prove he did it. The girl didn't get a look at her attacker. But after the accident he behaved in such a strange manner people began to ask questions and wonder if he wasn't guilty."

"Surely the girl would know better."

"Strangely, she was one of the first to accuse him—probably because he refused to visit her in the hospital and made no effort to see or speak to her again."

"But why?"

"He's never attempted to answer that in any satisfactory way beyond saying their friendship was a mistake." He paused. "A month after the episode he closed the California house and came back here. Later he had a real estate agent sell the house."

Victoria considered the story. "Have you ever talked to him about this? I can't picture Ernest doing such a cruel thing, anymore than I can think of him as being a murderer."

Will Grant's smile was bitter. "You hardly have an unprejudiced viewpoint. I'm afraid he's charmed you over to his side."

"You keep hinting at these terrible things," she said, with some anger. "But you haven't explained why. What reason could he possibly have to hurt the two women who meant the most to him following his wife's death?"

He looked at her directly. "I think he's insane."

"Insane!"

"It fits," the younger lawyer said.

"In what way?"

"This strangeness came over him after Elaine's death. The tragic loss of the beautiful woman he worshiped sent him into seclusion. But as the first pangs of grief left him, he became attracted to a pretty face. At first the romance blossomed, but then let us assume his twisted mind couldn't accept the thought of marriage with another woman, however attractive. He could not allow himself to marry this new love. And so the love turned to hatred and he tried to mar and destroy the beauty that had nearly tempted him into accepting Elaine's loss and beginning another normal relationship. It happened once in California, though the girl was lucky to survive, and it happened again with Stella. As soon as he realized it had come to the point where marriage must be considered, he did away with her."

She gave a startled gasp. "If what you say is true, he's too dangerous to be at large."

"Exactly. And since you appear to be his latest interest, I'd say the situation was especially perilous for you."

She listened to him in a daze. Everything else was forgotten as she tried to absorb this indictment of Ernest Collins. Even the accident tonight seemed unimportant beside these new revelations. Her desire to find the secret of her own beginnings was temporarily weakened by her concern for the young violinist.

At last she said, "Even if Ernest should seem the most likely suspect in each case, they still weren't able to prove his guilt." "That's so."

"Someone else could have attacked the girl in California and someone else could have shoved Stella over the cliff—if she was shoved. There are others living at Collins House, you know. What about Elizabeth, who has shut herself away from the world for eighteen years? Isn't she a good candidate? Or Roger Collins? He's a heavy drinker and known woman chaser!"

"The police are well aware of that," Will Grant said. "Otherwise I imagine Ernest would be in a prison cell today."

"And you think he should be!"

"I'm afraid so. I hope I'm wrong. I'd prefer to be wrong." She leaned back against the booth. "You've given me something to think about."

"After what you told me, I felt you had a right to know." Victoria smiled bitterly. "Now I'll be more unhappy at Collins House than before."

"You needn't be," he said. "You say you believe in Ernest. Perhaps you can somehow persuade him to prove his innocence to the rest of us."

At that moment Carolyn returned with Joe Haskell. She smiled down at them. "You two are having a great old talk," she said. "It's a shame to break it up, but I think it's time we started back."

Victoria gave a rueful laugh. "I didn't expect you to be the one to call a halt to the evening."

Carolyn looked at Will Grant slyly. "That was before Will turned on his charm," she said. And then she added, "Why don't you drive Victoria back in your car, Will? Then you can talk some more and Joe can come in the truck with me and you can bring him back to town."

Will stood up with a smile. "Why not?" he asked.

"It hardly seems necessary," Victoria said, caught-off guard by the other girl's bold suggestion. She knew it was a scheme of Carolyn's to have Joe to herself in the truck.

"But it will be fun!" Carolyn said with a laugh and grabbing Joe's arm started away. "We'll meet you at the house," she called back.

There was nothing to do but accept the situation. So shortly after Victoria found herself in the front seat of the sleek black car owned by Will Grant, heading along the narrow road to Collins House.

His handsome face was illuminated slightly by the reflection of the dash lights as he kept his eyes glued on the road ahead. "I hope you don't mind driving back with me," he said.

She smiled. "Not at all."

"I'm sorry," he went on, "if I upset you with my talk about Ernest. But I wanted to be perfectly honest with you. Collins House is a bleak old place and I don't relish the idea of your being ignorant of the dangers you may face there."

"I appreciate that," she said.

"And I have an ulterior motive," he went on, flashing her a smiling glance. "I think it would be very easy for me to fall in love with you myself."

CHAPTER 8

Elizabeth Stoddard was badly upset when she heard the news of the car accident the next morning. Victoria and Carolyn had managed to say goodnight to their companions and make their way into the old mansion and up to bed without attracting any attention. But in the morning there was no possibility of staving off the moment of truth any longer. Carolyn broke the news to her mother at breakfast and soon afterward Elizabeth summoned the two girls to the drawing room for a lecture.

As they sat quietly she paced back and forth in front of them. "It's not that I don't like Joe Haskell," she told Carolyn. "I think he's a fine boy with a good future at the plant. But I don't approve of your always meeting at a sordid place like the Blue Whale."

"You've never been there, Mother," Carolyn said plaintively. "How can you condemn it?"

"I've heard plenty about it," her mother assured her. "It's not the kind of place I want you to be seen in."

"All our friends go there!" Carolyn protested.

Victoria could see this did not impress Elizabeth and she felt Carolyn might do better for her cause if she did not try to press it so hard. For her own part she was still not fully recovered from the shock of the accident, and the story Will Grant had told her about Ernest last night had brought her a night of troubled dreams. Now in the sunshine of a new day it still took first place in a plague of troubles. She still thought that someone had tampered with the car before she took it out, but in the light of the news that Ernest might actually be an insane murderer it was a secondary matter.

The mistress of Collins House turned her attention to her. "I am sorry you had to suffer another shocking experience while a member of this household," she said. "I wouldn't blame you for wanting to desert us."

"I can hardly blame anyone here," Victoria said. "The car failed."

As she spoke she saw Carolyn suddenly lower her eyes and study the carpet as if she feared being dragged into the discussion. Again she wondered whether the teen-ager was truly her friend and if she knew more than she pretended.

"None the less I feel responsible for you while you are in my employ," the attractive older woman said. "It was wrong of Carolyn to involve you in her wild pranks." She turned to her daughter. "You say you have already notified the garage man?"

"He's coming for it this morning with his tow truck," Carolyn said. "I asked him to stop by the house and report the damage."

"From what you tell me it must be a complete wreck!" Elizabeth said.

"I'd say it was," her daughter admitted.

"And you can be lucky your lifeless body is not in it," Elizabeth reproached her. "You've been driving too much and too recklessly. No wonder the car failed. You've abused it."

"That's not so," Carolyn said petulantly, standing up. "Morgan checks it and I've taken it into the village regularly for repairs."

Her mother regarded her coldly. "It may be some time before you have another, if this one can't be put in shape."

"I knew you'd be unfair!" Carolyn cried out between anger and tears. And she turned and ran out of the drawing room and upstairs.

Her mother sighed. "She can be a difficult child when she likes," she said for Victoria's benefit. "I regret making you a party to such a scene."

"I can understand your being upset," she said placatingly. "But I can also see Carolyn's side of it. She's very young and it is lonely here. The car has been her chief source of pleasure."

Elizabeth's handsome face lost some of its anger. "I suppose you're right," she said with a hint of weariness. "I won't keep you any longer. It's time to get on with David's morning work."

The boy was so excited about the news of the wrecked car that Victoria had a hard time getting him settled down to his regular studies. He sat in the easy chair across the desk from her and kept asking question after question.

She studied his eager, boyish face and with a resigned smile said, "I've told you everything at least twice. Must you continue to harp on the accident?"

David looked at her slyly. "Maybe I know something that you don't!"

Victoria couldn't be sure what he meant. He might be bluffing her. He frequently told tall stories to make himself important. She said, "Now what are you trying to say?"

"Matt Morgan must have known there was something wrong with the car. I saw him stretched out on the floor underneath it yesterday. He was pounding at something near the front of it."

She frowned. "I hope you're not making that up, David."

He showed defiance. "I did see Morgan under Carolyn's car and he was repairing something. So there!"

"You're sure it was yesterday afternoon you saw him?"

"Yes." Victoria hesitated.

"Well, it doesn't make any difference now. Please get on with your history studies." She didn't want him to know how much importance his words had for her. And she made up her mind that as soon as the study period was over she'd go out to the garage and question Morgan. If he had a reasonable explanation for David's story, no harm would be done. If he denied it she would know that either he or the boy was lying.

Time seemed to pass at a deadly slow pace but finally the lesson period ended and she dismissed David to take his usual run outside before luncheon. As soon as she'd straightened out the books, she left the library and headed directly for the garage.

Matt Morgan was standing in the open garage door along with another man in the blue uniform and cap of a service station attendant. As Victoria drew near them, the two men stopped what was apparently a serious discussion and turned to greet her with questioning glances.

She felt a little awkward but was determined to query Morgan. The big, burly man looked unhappy at her sudden appearance.

He said, "Yes, miss? Something I can do for you?"

"There is," she said. "I wanted to ask you about the car that went out of control last night. I was driving it, as you've probably heard."

The other man took on a startled expression and spoke up. "You were the one at the wheel? You were lucky, miss. I just came from looking at her now. She's a complete wreck. I just got through makin' a report to Mrs. Stoddard."

Victoria thought it would do no harm to ask the garage man a pertinent question. "Have you any idea what happened to the steering?"

"The tie rod went," he said. Including Morgan in his glance, he went on, "I never seen anything exactly like it. Craziest kind of wear I ever seen on a tie rod. It just popped out of place and then you had no control. Almost looked like it had been bent, but of course it hadn't."

"Did you know the steering wasn't right on the car?" Victoria asked Morgan.

The burly man seemed uneasy. "No. Why should I?"

"David says he saw you working underneath the car yesterday afternoon. He says you were pounding at something."

Matt Morgan's jaw dropped open. He looked at the garage man with a guilty expression before he turned to her and said, "Well, what if I was? The exhaust pipe was loose and I fixed it."

The garage man chuckled. "If you'd known the whole car was going to the junk heap today, you could have saved yourself a lot of trouble," he told Morgan. "I got to be getting on." He tipped his cap to her. "Safe driving, miss!" And with another chuckle he went out to his truck and got in it and drove away.

Victoria watched the tow truck go and then she turned to Morgan again. "So it was the exhaust pipe you were working at? And you didn't notice anything wrong with the tie rod then?"

His stem face was a mask of belligerence. "No," he said. "You trying to put the blame on me? It won't work!"

She studied him calmly. "I'm not trying to blame anyone, Morgan. I hoped that you might help me find out the truth." She turned and went back to the house.

The day passed uneventfully. She busied herself with David and in her free time kept as much to herself as possible. Carolyn was depressed over her wrecked car and her mother's refusal to consider replacing it. Roger Collins had gone off to Ellsworth in his own sedan early in the morning and Victoria hadn't seen him before he left.

She kept thinking of what Will Grant had told her and worrying about Ernest. She still clung to the belief that Ernest was perfectly sane and not guilty of any of the crimes of which he had been suspected. She knew the mounting evidence was all against him but she put her faith in her instincts. And they told her Ernest was an unhappy but honorable young man.

Evening came and Carolyn insisted on sharing her room again. Victoria reluctantly agreed but told the girl there would be no need to continue the arrangement another night. And she felt this to be true. Her nerves were in much better shape and there was only a slight tenderness around the small wound on her head to remind her of the strange events in the cellar.

Carolyn seemed attracted to the painting Ernest had left in the room. Just before going to bed she strolled slowly over to study it. "It's really good," she said. "Have you ever seen the view from the captain's walk?"

"No," Victoria admitted. She was sitting on the side of her bed combing her hair.

Carolyn was staring at the painting again. "You must go up there and take a look one day soon. Then you'll appreciate how realistic this painting is."

"Ernest seems to think it is something special," she said.

The other girl turned and nodded wisely. "Naturally. He was in love with Stella."

Victoria hesitated in her combing. "So I understand. If it hadn't been for the accident, they might have married, I suppose."

Carolyn walked back to her cot. "I don't think so," she said. "Ernest told me once he intended to remain faithful to the memory of Elaine. He said he didn't want to marry again ever."

She found the girl's quiet statement a startling endorsement of Will Grant's theory. But she did not want to believe it. She said, "He may have felt that way once, but time often changes people's mind. Don't you agree?"

The other girl slipped between the sheets of the cot. "Not Ernest. He's a strange sort of person. I guess all musicians are temperamental. And he's gone through so much." Carolyn yawned.

Victoria made no reply, though her face wore a troubled look as she reached to switch off the bed lamp. And she tossed and turned in bed for a long while before being able to sleep.

The following day was wet and miserable. Tension in the old mansion ran high. Roger began the day drinking and continued until he retired early. David was restless and unhappy because it was too rainy to play outside and Carolyn was still sulking about getting a new car. Elizabeth seemed strangely pale and withdrawn and Victoria noticed her going down to the cellar in mid-afternoon. She was carrying a large package in her arms and did not come back up again for more than an hour. Victoria happened to be in the corridor when she finally did return and the older woman chose to ignore her as she walked by.

Thursday brought sunshine again and it was much warmer than it had been. With the improvement in the weather the old house seemed less baleful and everyone's spirits appeared to rise. Roger bustled off to attend to his duties at the cannery and Carolyn, who had finally persuaded her mother there was an excellent buy offered in a new car at the Collinsport garage, drove gleefully to the village to inspect the bargain.

David had one of his good days with his studies and so Victoria found herself free early in the afternoon. The house was quiet and she went up to her own room. Carolyn's cot was gone; she would be remaining in her own room from now on. Victoria deposited several of the lesson books she'd brought upstairs with her on the dresser and then went over and opened the casement windows.

The stimulating salt tang of the air refreshed her and she stood there for a long moment looking out at the cliffs and the sea beyond. The ripple of breeze caressed her long dark hair and sent a wandering wisp of it across her forehead. She decided she might take a walk since there might not be many warm days like this left. As she crossed the room the painting caught her attention and she remembered Carolyn's advice that she should go up to the captain's walk and see the view for herself one day. She suddenly had the impulse to make the visit up there right away. It would be an ideal afternoon for it. The skies were clear and she could probably see as far as the village. In the hall she decided the small flight of stairs leading to the next level would be the first step in her journey to the roof.

When she reached the upper corridor it only took her a minute to discover the door that concealed the narrow winding stairway to the captain's walk. She mounted the worn wooden steps and finally emerged in the railed area with its ornate roof.

She leaned against the railing, grasping it with both hands as she stared at the majestic view surrounding her on all sides.

It was truly a beautiful sight. Not only did the captain's walk offer a commanding view of the ocean but she could see for miles up and down the coast. The village of Collinsport looked like a collection of toy white houses clustered around the small bay. The great dark buildings of the cannery rose high above the wharves and there were the masts of the fishing schooners looking like a nest of toothpicks.

She could understand why this exciting vista had caught Stella's fancy and why Ernest thought so much of the painting she'd done of it. She made up her mind to study it again when she returned downstairs. Lost in her appreciation of the lovely scene she did not realize there was someone coming up the winding stairs until she heard footsteps almost directly behind her. She whirled around, startled, and saw a smiling Roger Collins standing there.

"I noticed you were up here when I drove in," he said. "I decided you ought to have a guide to point out the places of interest."

She managed a smile. "I've been doing very well, thanks." She'd had a strange feeling toward the blond man since the accident with the car. She still wondered if his being in the garage could have had anything to do with it.

"I remember coming up here when I wasn't more than four or five," Roger said, joining her at the railing and studying the ocean. "I thought this was the top of the world then. The Empire State Building of Maine." He sighed. "It doesn't seem so high or so thrilling now. We lose a lot when we cast off the illusions of childhood. But it's still a fine view."

"I couldn't agree more," she said.

"I lived in Augusta for quite a few years," Roger said. "Perhaps more than anything else I missed the ocean."

"I can understand that," she said. "I think David is more contented here now."

"I give you full credit for that," the blond man said. "You're doing wonders with him."

"He's a very intelligent boy," she said. Suddenly Roger slipped his arm around her waist and exerted some pressure to draw her toward him.

Now he looked down at her with smiling consideration. "I hope you're happy here, Victoria."

"I am," she said, trying to move away from him and yet not make it seem too obvious. "And of course I value the freedom this job gives me." She stressed the freedom in the hope he would take the hint and release her, but he showed no sign of doing this.

"I'm a very lonely man these days, Victoria," he said with such a solemn tone it was almost a mockery. "There are times when I feel the need of the advice an intelligent young girl like you might offer me."

"I'll be glad to offer you advice any time," she said with a touch of desperation, pulling away from him sharply.

He let her go and stared at her with crimson rising in his cheeks. "You're not very friendly," he said.

"I don't enjoy being pawed or followed around," she told him indignantly.

"You're making a mistake, Victoria," he said. "You may need my friendship before you leave this house."

"I'm quite willing to be friends on any reasonable basis. I think the way you've acted just now is insulting."

He laughed unpleasantly. "Your appearance often deceives me. I think of you as a sophisticated young woman, but you're really only a sheltered little refugee from a foundling home."

"I'm not ashamed of my upbringing," she said. "And I understand you were similarly confused about Mary Gordon and the other governesses before me, who had to leave because of your annoying them."

She saw that she had scored a point with this. He looked startled but he quickly recovered his usual bland assurance. "It seems I have won myself a reputation," he said. "I'll have to try and live up to it."

"Don't exert yourself for me," she said. "I'm willing to forget this, but I don't want any more of the same."

He shrugged. "Just as you say, Victoria. But it's too bad. A pity you are interested in Ernest, rather than me. I'm a much better bet."

"Who says I'm interested in Ernest?"

Roger looked very pleased with himself. "No one has to say anything, my dear. You've shown it plainly ever since you came here."

"In any case, it's none of your business."

"But it is," he insisted. "I like you, Victoria. I wouldn't want to see you get hurt."

She decided the conversation had gone on long enough, so she started for the stairway. Roger stepped in front of her and blocked the way.

"I want to leave," she said impatiently.

"Not until we discuss Cousin Ernest."

"There's nothing to discuss!"

"I'll give you a warning. Playing the romantic game with him can be more dangerous than you imagine. And it will get you nothing!"

Victoria found her anger mounting. "I don't want to hear any of this," she told him.

"It will get you nothing," he repeated in an even tone. "And you might even wind up like poor Stella!" He began to laugh harshly.

"You're a monster!" she cried angrily as he continued to laugh and stepped aside for her to hurry down the narrow stairs. She didn't stop until she had reached the bottom, his taunting laughter still echoing in her ears.

She was still quivering with anger when she reached her room. When she opened the door and went in she was startled to find Elizabeth standing in there. The mistress of Collins House was wearing one of the smart black dresses that made her look taller and more slender than she really was. She was staring at Stella's painting with her back to Victoria. Hearing her enter the room she turned with a smile on her patrician face.

"I hope you'll forgive this intrusion," she apologized. "I wanted to take a look at the painting again."

Victoria made an effort to hide her upset state. "Not at all," she said.

Elizabeth studied her closely. "You're very pale," she said. "You look actually ill. Are you all right?"

She nodded. "Yes. I was feeling slightly ill but I'm fine now."

"You should get more rest," the older woman said. "I suppose Carolyn has been keeping you awake until all hours with her chattering. You're probably glad that's over."

Victoria smiled. "I enjoyed her."

The other woman glanced at the painting again. I'm glad Ernest managed to hold on to this. It's the only one of Stella's paintings here."

"Did she do a lot of work?"

Elizabeth nodded. "She was always busy at one painting or another. But when her parents came to get her things at the cottage they took everything with them." She sighed. "I had no chance to speak with them. We were all so shocked and they were feeling so bad."

"Of course," she said.

"Stella was fond of this place," Elizabeth said, starting for the door. "She often said she'd like to spend all her life here." She paused and gave Victoria a sad glance. "And, of course, that was how it turned out," she said.

Victoria could find nothing to say in reply as Elizabeth nodded and went out, closing the door after her. Feeling thoroughly shaken, she sank into the easy chair by the open casement window and stared off into space. It was a strange house, filled with strange people, and she had deliberately come to live among them for her own reasons.

But did the reasons make sense any longer? Would she be wise to put all her hopes and curiosity to one side and run from the somber old mansion while there was still time? But that would mean deserting Ernest and David! Surely they both needed her.

Yet she was now certain that within these ancient walls an enemy stalked her—an enemy who had attempted to take her life and who would surely strike again. As long as she remained at Collins House the shadow was over her. What good would it do either Ernest or young David if she stayed on for their sakes and was murdered as a result? But then, Will Grant was insisting the murderer in Collins House was Ernest himself.

She at last got up from the chair and began mechanically changing and washing for dinner. It seemed best to try to clear her mind of all doubts and worries and attempt to live for the moment while she remained in the weird old house on Widow's Hill. Having come to this minor decision, she felt a little better. Because it was a pleasant, rather warm night she decided to wear a smart summer dress, hoping it wouldn't catch Roger's attention and start him bothering her again.

As it turned out he was on model behavior at dinner. Both Elizabeth and Carolyn complimented her on the dress, and she relaxed and began to enjoy herself a little. Carolyn was in high spirits because her mother had agreed to the car, so all seemed to be well once more.

Dinner was hardly over when Will Grant's sleek black sedan appeared in the gravel driveway before the main entrance. Elizabeth hurried to let him in and the tall young lawyer spoke pleasantly to Victoria and Carolyn, who were standing just inside the drawing room. Then he went on out to the library for a private conference with the older woman.

As the library door closed after them, Victoria turned to the other girl and asked, "Does he come here often in the evenings?"

"Generally about twice a week," she said. "There are always legal papers to be signed and contracts to be approved." She smiled. "You know Mother is very sharp about money. She keeps a close eye on the business."

"I'd expect your Uncle Roger would do more."

"Uncle Roger!" Carolyn laughed. "He's a darling but he hasn't any business head. Mother found that out a long time ago."

Carolyn went out to the garage to talk to Morgan about the new car she was buying and Victoria decided she would take a stroll around the front of the house. She had no desire to talk with the surly handyman. She passed Will Grant's car and walked toward the edge of the cliff. Turning to stare at the house, once again she was impressed by its size. Elizabeth had mentioned forty rooms, but she wondered if there weren't actually more. The east wing that had been closed so long appeared to have half that many and then there was a rear section, not so large, that had been shut off since Ernest had abandoned his apartment in it for a room in the main building. She turned and walked slowly toward the cliff and the footpath that followed it.

She had only gone a few steps when she heard someone coming up swiftly behind her. She turned to see a smiling Will Grant striding towards her. He wore a fawn sport jacket and dark brown trousers.

"I was beginning to think I wouldn't catch up with you," he said, a little short of breath.

"You should have called out. I'd have waited," she smiled. His eyes twinkled. "I didn't dare risk it."

"What a wonderful night," she said, as they began to stroll along the path side by side.

"Even makes Collins House and Widow's Hill pleasant places," he said. "Have you recovered from the other night?"

"More or less," she told him. "Things keep happening."

He gave her a sharp glance. "What kind of things?"

"Like Roger Collins trying to be a little too friendly."

Will Grant's bronzed face showed anger. "Did you complain to Elizabeth? She'll soon settle him."

She laughed. "I think I managed very well without bothering her. She has enough other troubles. Poor woman!"

"I agree," Will said. "And I don't think she's been too well lately. Several times when I've come here she's seemed strangely tense. It's not like her to show nervousness and yet she has. A couple of times I've felt she was on the brink of telling me something and then she backed away from it."

They had come to the high point of the cliffs and she halted and looked up at him with serious eyes. "You think she has some sort of secret? Something that's troubling her?"

He nodded. "I'd say so. Yes."

"Do you think the secret has anything to do with Ernest?"

"I've wondered. Frankly, it wouldn't surprise me." Victoria sighed and looked away. "I've thought of what you said the other night, I can't make myself believe what you told me about him."

"Stella had the same kind of faith in him." He nodded toward the jagged rocks down below with the waves breaking over them. "She ended on those rocks."

"I still feel you're making a mistake in blaming him," she said.

"I'd like to change your mind."

She looked up at him again. "You may be on the wrong track completely. This secret you believe Elizabeth is keeping to herself may have nothing to do with Ernest's guilt or innocence. It may be connected with something quite different. Have you considered that?"

He shrugged. "No. I suppose it's possible."

"You're obsessed with the idea that Ernest is a killer and insane," she said. "It makes me begin to wonder if you aren't the twisted one."

Will looked startled. "Me?"

"As far as Stella's death is concerned, you could be a suspect yourself. You admit you and she were good friends. You drive in and out of here often. And you may have made up the story about that girl who was attacked in Santa Barbara."

"I might have, but I didn't," he protested. "Are you trying to prove I was the one who murdered Stella?"

"I'm trying to show you how easy it is to build circumstantial evidence and suspect anyone," she told him. "And when it comes to that, Stella may not have been murdered at all. She could have taken a dizzy spell, fainted or even stumbled."

Will Grant smiled at her wryly. "I wish I had a defender like you. Ernest doesn't know how lucky he is. When is he due back?"

"The middle of next week," she said.

"You'll be glad to see him?"

"Why not?" She said it with a smile but there was no smile in her heart or mind. She'd heard so much since he left. In spite of her brave front she couldn't help having doubts. There would be questions she'd have to ask him and she wasn't sure that she could hope for satisfactory answers.

The young lawyer said, "You'll find out more then."

"Yes," she agreed slowly. "I'll find out more then." And they started back toward Collins House.

CHAPTER 9

In the days that followed before Ernest's return from his midwestern concert tour, Will Grant came to Collins House twice. Victoria saw him on both occasions and the second time accepted his invitation to go for a drive in his car. It was another of the pleasant fall evenings and he had come over early after dinner to confer with Elizabeth and have some documents signed.

Victoria was sitting reading in the drawing room when he and Elizabeth came down the hallway from the library and he paused on his way out to suggest she go with him for a short ride. It was a tempting offer, but she hesitated, not knowing just how Elizabeth might feel about it.

The mistress of Collins House was standing in the background, taking it all in and not looking too pleased. "I don't imagine you'll have much time to enjoy the countryside," was her comment. "It will be dark very soon."

Will Grant smiled. "We'll have a half-hour at least. I haven't shown Victoria the shore road and there's some excellent scenery along it."

Victoria decided to risk offending her employer and said, "I'd enjoy it. But I don't want to be gone long. I have a lot of reading to catch up on."

Will showed his pleasure. "Lots of time for reading when the snow comes," he said. "We won't get too many more perfect evenings like this." As they started out, he turned to Elizabeth and added, "It would do you a world of good to come with us. Why don't you consider it?"

The lovely older woman looked aghast. "You know I never go out, Will."

"And I still say you'd be better off if you did."

"You two go along," Elizabeth said quickly. "Just don't be too late, Victoria."

When they were in the car and starting out toward the main road, Victoria asked him, "You didn't really think Elizabeth would join us? You must have invited her as a joke."

Will was busy guiding the car along the narrow, wooded road. "Not entirely," he said. "I've tried to talk her into leaving the house before and of course it hasn't worked. But I intend to keep asking her from time to time. Sooner or later she'll have to give up this sick business of remaining in the house for years on end."

"She's so normal in most other ways," Victoria said. "She can't really believe that missing husband of hers would expect her to keep such a vigil."

"I think she stayed there alone in the beginning because she was deeply hurt," he suggested, keeping his eyes on the road. "And of course she's always hoped her husband would come back. Now it's gotten to be a crazy kind of pattern that she hesitates to break."

"It's almost as if she's afraid of something being discovered if she leaves," Victoria said with a frown. "As if she's concealing something and can't leave the house because of it."

"I hadn't thought of it in that way."

"Now that I've been in the house long enough to be familiar with its routine, I'm noticing more things," Victoria said. "It seems to me Elizabeth makes an unusual number of trips to the cellar area and sometimes she stays down there a long time."

The young lawyer's face showed interest. He gave her a quick glance. "What reason does there seem to be for these visits?"

"I've never heard her mention any," she said. "Maybe she has an extra storage room down there. I've noticed she often takes things down with her."

Will braked the car as they came to the junction with the main highway. "You had one unpleasant experience down there in the east wing area."

She shuddered. "I don't even want to think about that."

"Would you say she tries to avoid attention when she makes these various trips to the cellar? Or does she go about them quite openly?"

"I'd say she tries to avoid attracting attention," Victoria told him. "On more than one occasion she has deliberately ignored me when I've met her coming up. And she's usually very agreeable."

"Sounds as if you might have hit on something."

"And lately she's been tense and restless," she recalled. "Several times she's mentioned Ernest to me and said how relieved she would be when he returns."

Will's eyebrows raised. "Probably she's worried about him."

"It could be that," she agreed. "But I have the impression something at Collins House is troubling her and she is waiting for him to return to discuss it with him."

"Perhaps," the young lawyer said reluctantly. "On the other hand, she knows what a strain traveling and doing all those concerts must be for Ernest and she's probably wondering how he is managing."

They swung off the main highway and drove along the shore road which was as scenic as he had promised. But Elizabeth had been right. By the time they had driven only a short distance darkness was descending and the best of the view was spoiled. Will apologized and stopped at a turnout overlooking a point of land with a tall white lighthouse whose beam was already sweeping the bay so they could watch it.

"I've always been fascinated by lighthouses," he said. "I'd probably have been happier as a lighthouse keeper than I am as a lawyer."

She laughed. "It must be a lonely life. And if you lived in the lighthouse the quarters would be terribly small. Especially for a man with a wife and family. And you would want a wife and family, wouldn't you?"

He shrugged. "I want them now, but I haven't got them."

"That's your own fault."

He shook his head. "I wouldn't say that. It's merely that I haven't been able to meet the right girl."

She smiled at him. "Perhaps you should visit the Blue Whale more often. Carolyn considers it a haven of romance."

"Carolyn and I have widely varying views about many things," he said. "And especially about the Blue Whale."

"There must be some eligible young women in the area."

"Plenty. But none I could live with."

"Maybe you're too fussy," she suggested.

"I do admit to being particular," he said. "But I have no doubts where you're concerned. Why don't you forget Ernest and think about marrying me?"

Victoria gave an incredulous little laugh. "Is this the spot where you make all your proposals?"

"My first," he said. "And that's the truth. What about it,

Victoria?"

She waited a moment before she answered. Then she said slowly, "Let's try being friends for a while. Will. I'm a little confused where romance is concerned these days."

"Even after all I've told you about Ernest, you're still in love with him?"

"I still care for him," she said. "When he comes back I'll decide whether it's love or not."

"I see," he said. "Well, I can always keep on trying."

"I'd be heartbroken if you didn't," she said. "Especially since you go about it in a much nicer way than Roger Collins."

"Roger!" he groaned. "There's not a pretty girl in this part of the state he hasn't made a play for."

"I suppose I should be pleased to be included," she laughed. "But I could have skipped the honor."

"There is one thing I must warn you about," Will said, all seriousness again. "It's one of the reasons I wanted us to have this drive together tonight."

Victoria's curiosity was aroused by the gravity of his tone. "What?" she asked.

"When Ernest returns, don't press him with a lot of questions about what I've told you."

She frowned. "I must be honest with him. I want to hear his side of it."

"I realize that," the young lawyer said. "But you must allow for his mental state. He's in no shape to withstand a barrage of questions."

"How else can I find out the truth?"

"The truth may not be as important as your own safety," Will said with a harsh note in his voice. "I wouldn't have revealed what I did if I'd thought you were going to run back to him with it. You don't want to wind up like Stella, do you?"

"Do you think there's any risk of that?"

"There might be if you close in on Ernest with a lot of questions he can't or won't answer. Try to be patient. Discuss it a little at a time."

Victoria stared at him through the shadows that filled the car's front seat. In a voice close to a whisper she said, "You think he's really insane, don't you? You think he killed that girl and nothing will change your mind."

"I'm afraid not," he said solemnly. "And from what you've said about Elizabeth's behavior I'm beginning to wonder if she doesn't believe the same thing—if she's not hiding some evidence that could convict him."

"She could be an accomplice, when it comes to that," she said with a touch of derision in her tone. "Or even the murderess herself! But I don't believe she is either of those things." The beam from the lighthouse made one of its regular sweeps in their direction, illuminating the front seat of the car for a moment so that she could see the real concern on his handsome face. Then the beam moved on and they were in darkness once more.

Will spoke in a low voice. "What a quixotic little fool you are," he said. "And how much I want to protect you!" He drew her to him for a tender embrace. The kiss lasted for a long moment and she accepted it as sincere and loving. There was no hint of the coarse passion Roger had displayed in Will Grant's approach and she realized many girls would consider themselves fortunate to have a man of his qualities ask them to marry him. So might she under other circumstances. But even in the moment when her lips met his, she could picture Ernest's sensitive, unhappy face.

He let her go and turned abruptly to the wheel. "I must get you back," he said. "We both promised Elizabeth."

She knew it was his way of covering up an awkward moment. She settled back against the seat, her eyes on the lighthouse, whose beam was now stretching out over the bay. "It is late," she agreed. "But I enjoyed it."

When they drove back to Collins House she saw there was a light in the drawing room and also upstairs in Carolyn's bedroom. Darkness cloaked the imposing old mansion and its grounds, but there was a large full moon to dispel the gloom. Will Grant saw her to the door and for a moment held her hand in his, as if loath to let her go.

"Ernest is due back tomorrow or the next day, isn't he?" he said.

She nodded. "Unless there is some delay."

"Remember what I said," he warned.

"I will."

"I have to be in Boston for a convention," he said. "I'll be back by the weekend and I'll make a point to come by. I'll be bringing Elizabeth a report, anyway." He paused. "If you should need me in the meantime, the office can tell you where to reach me."

They kissed very briefly again and she went inside. Elizabeth must have been watching from the drawing room window, because the moment Victoria entered the foyer the attractive older woman came out to greet her.

"I'm glad you got back in a reasonable time," she said. "I worry when anyone is out late." Her expression showed that she had seen the kiss of a moment before. "Did you have a nice time? Will can be charming when he likes."

"It was very pleasant," Victoria said quietly.

"Of course, you mustn't put too much stock in what he says."

"Oh?" Victoria registered polite surprise. She could tell that the other woman had been displeased with what she saw. But she felt that Elizabeth had no right to be spying on her or offering an opinion of her friends.

"Will likes to hear himself talk," she went on. "And he's a dreadful flirt. I've even had to warn Carolyn against him, young as she is. No doubt he went out of his way to impress you."

"He seemed to behave very naturally," she said, starting for the stairs.

"Just don't count too much on anything he may have said," Elizabeth warned her. "I feel I owe it to you to tell you that."

Victoria hesitated on the second step. "Thank you," she said in the same cool, polite tone.

"I respect Will's talents as a lawyer or I wouldn't have him in charge of the firm's affairs," Elizabeth went on primly. "But I also am aware of his weaknesses as a man." The older woman smiled in a thin manner. "Good night, Victoria."

"Good night, Mrs. Stoddard," she said with a touch of weariness, and hurried on upstairs. She was annoyed at the deliberate way Elizabeth had tried to turn her against Will Grant. Why had she warned her to discount Will's words? Surely because she was afraid the young lawyer would reveal too many of the family secrets.

By the time she reached the second floor, the light in Carolyn's room had been turned off, she could tell, since it did not shine through under her door. She had considered going in to chat with the teen-ager for a moment, but now decided to go straight to bed.

She had left one of the casement windows open in her own room and it was pleasantly cool and filled with fresh air. She stood at the window for a moment studying the great yellow moon and thinking how wonderful it would be to have Ernest back under the same roof again. With a happy expression on her pretty face she shut the windows and began to prepare for bed.

She realized that Will had offered her good advice. While she wanted with all her heart to believe that Ernest was innocent of any crime there was still the small chance that he might be mentally ill and a killer. It would be best to follow Will's suggestion and only broach a little of what she'd heard at a time. It shouldn't take long for the violinist to betray himself in some way if he were in the wrong.

Perhaps that was why Elizabeth didn't want her talking with Will Grant. She might know the young lawyer's feelings about Ernest and be afraid of his telling her too much. It could be that Elizabeth was mixed up more deeply in the dark happenings at Collins House than anyone guessed. And it had been Elizabeth who had sent that letter to the foundling home offering her a position. Victoria still questioned her motives for doing this.

Sleep came readily. But she woke with a start to discover the room still in darkness. She had the feeling she had just slept a short time and that she had been roused from the depths of an early slumber by some intruding sound.

Sitting up in bed, she stared into the black shadows, hearing only the distant wash of the waves. Then it came! The eerie scratching noise she'd heard in the room on that other night and also in the storage room in the east wing cellar the day she had been attacked. Her flesh fairly crept as the weird scratching continued and then she thought she heard a deep sigh.

She had left her dressing gown on a chair to the right of the four-poster and now she reached for it as she swung out of bed. Throwing it on, she retreated fearfully to the other side of the room putting as much distance between herself and the ghostly noises as she could.

The moon had gone down or was under clouds and so no revealing light filtered through the curtains. The room was like a sealed pit. Victoria was shivering with fright and as she edged slowly toward the door and escape she heard the shuffling sound that invariably came next. It had been on the heels of this that she had been attacked the other day and so she was doubly terrified.

As the shuffling came toward her, she made a frantic dash to the door, slid back the bolt and rushed out into the hallway. She scarcely felt any safer as the night light had been turned off and the hall also was in darkness. On an impulse she rushed to Carolyn's door and pounded on it as loudly as she could and screamed for help.

"Carolyn! Wake up! It's Victoria! Let me in!" She kept repeating the words in a panic, expecting at each moment the shuffling to follow her into the hall and terrified that the horror must finally close in on her as it had before.

Her heart was pounding madly; her breathing came in frenzied gasps. She continued to scream and pound on the door, gazing over her shoulder with fear-glazed eyes, expecting each second would reveal her pursuer.

Then she heard Carolyn's sleepy answer from the other side of the door and a second later the light came on inside the room. Victoria uttered a small moan of gratitude and still pressed against the door. Next the bolt was slid back and Carolyn swung open the door.

"Whatever is wrong?" the teenager gasped.

Victoria quickly stepped inside and closed and bolted the door. "Something in my room! The same shuffling I heard in the cellar!"

"Did you see anything?"

She opened her eyes and looked at the teenager. "No. I didn't wait! I managed to get to the door."

Carolyn's pretty face was ashen with fright. "What will we do?"

Her answer was provided by the sound of voices in the hall. Victoria realized she must have wakened everyone with her hysterical outburst. In spite of her fear she began to also feel some embarrassment.

Turning to Carolyn she said, "I hear your mother and Roger. I'd better open the door and explain." She went to the door again and when she opened it Elizabeth was standing there with an angry expression on her patrician face with a sleepy-eyed Roger at her elbow. Both were in dressing gowns and had obviously just gotten out of their beds.

Elizabeth demanded, "What's been going on here?"

"I had a bad scare," Victoria said in a voice still shaky. "Someone or something came into my room."

"Didn't you have the door bolted?" the older woman asked.

"Yes. But they must have come in some other way."

Roger Collins snorted. "Are you certain you haven't been dreaming all this?"

"It surely sounds like a nightmare," Elizabeth said sharply. Looking toward her room, she added, "I suppose I'd better take a look, anyway, to make sure."

"Be careful. Mother!" Carolyn pleaded from behind Victoria.

Her mother gave her a crushing glance. Flinging open the door of Victoria's room, Elizabeth marched into the darkness. Victoria followed a few steps and then the older woman found the bed lamp and switched it on. As the room flooded with its soft yellow glow she glanced around and commented, "Your phantom seems to have vanished as quickly as it came."

"I know I heard something," Victoria insisted as she grew more ashamed and uneasy. Her own survey of the room showing it to be empty as well.

Carolyn and Roger were standing in the doorway. "Your imagination is too vivid, Victoria," he said with a nasty grin. "You seem to have trouble with it both day and night."

"I'm sure Victoria didn't make all that fuss for nothing," Carolyn said defensively. "If she says she heard something, I believe her!"

Elizabeth gave her a reproving look. "We appreciate your loyalty to Victoria, but you really shouldn't encourage her in this nonsense."

"No wonder she's afraid! I don't blame her," Carolyn went on angrily. "She could have been killed in the cellar the other day."

Elizabeth moved across to the door. "This is hardly the time for such discussions," she snapped. "We'll go into this in the morning. Meanwhile, Victoria, I suggest you try to get some more rest. It might be wise for you to leave the bed lamp on all night, if your nerves are so bad."

"I will," Victoria said with as much dignity as she could muster. "I'm sorry I disturbed you all. I was sure I heard something."

"It's all right," Elizabeth said rather impatiently and started out with the others going ahead.

Victoria was about to close the door after them when her eyes fastened on the wall directly across from her and she saw something that made her freeze with horror. In a stricken voice she called out, "Wait!"

Elizabeth was the first to return. She came over to the ashen-faced Victoria with her bewilderment clearly showing. "What is it now?"

She swallowed hard and pointed a trembling hand to Stella's painting. "Look!"

As the older woman did so, she gasped. "I can't believe it!" she said.

Carolyn and Roger had come into the room and were now staring at the painting as well. "It's ruined!" Carolyn said.

"Rotten bit of vandalism," was Roger Collins' disgusted comment. Someone had savagely ripped the canvas so that it was impossible to decipher any of its original pattern.

"I knew someone had come in here," Victoria said.

Elizabeth turned on her angrily. "I quite agree that someone came in here, but not in the way you describe. I suspect this was done earlier this evening when you were out driving." She made it sound as if Victoria had done a very wrong thing in going out with Will Grant.

She at once protested. "No. It couldn't have been. I would have noticed it before I went to bed. Just as I did now, in spite of being upset."

"In the dim light of this room's single lamp?" Elizabeth questioned her. "I doubt that very much. I don't think this painting was attacked by any ghostly hand. I've seen something like this damage before. I'm reasonably sure who's to blame."

Carolyn gave her mother a frightened glance. "Not David!"

Her mother nodded grimly. "David! He's been behaving entirely too well lately. I've been waiting for something like this — though I must say I hadn't expected him to come up here to practice his maliciousness."

Roger looked shaken. "If the boy did that, I'll trounce him myself," he mumbled. "I've a good mind to go to his room now."

"It can wait until morning," Elizabeth said sternly. "We have all lost enough rest. Time enough to face this unpleasantness then."

Again Victoria was left alone in the room. This time she closed and bolted the door. She walked slowly across to the painting and examined it closely. It seemed to have been slashed with a razor or even a sharp knife, a very sharp knife! The keen edge had done its work well. Whoever had attacked the painting must have done so in a frenzy of rage. There was nothing left to hint of the beauty it had once portrayed.

She turned away from it filled with a nausea combined of shock and fear. Sinking into the easy chair, she stared straight head of her as she tried to fathom out the meaning of what had happened. Elizabeth had been quick to point a finger of suspicion. Too quick! She was more than ever suspicious of the mistress of Collins House.

Without a doubt David would deny the vandalism and whether the others chose to believe his denial or not, she was certain he was not to blame—just as she was certain she had heard the phantom make its way into her room. Yet, as Elizabeth had said, the door was locked and bolted at the time. So the entry must have been made by some other means.

She glanced about the room, studying the wall, trying to decide where the sound had first come from. It had seemed to center on a spot midway along the left wall and she saw that in this area the wall had wood paneling halfway up it. With sudden excitement she rose quickly and went over to examine the section.

She studied the shining oak panels and touched their uneven surface with her fingers. She hoped to find some sign of a hidden door or even a small panel that would open, but she was doomed to disappointment. The wall seemed especially solid. The paneling seemed to have been constructed of thick oak timbers.

At last she gave up in despair. Even though she was sleepy, she felt she could not trust herself in the four-poster again. Instead, she carefully arranged the easy chair facing the wall where she'd heard the noise, and after lining it with blankets, settled down in it for the night. She intended to leave the bed lamp on and she doubted that she'd get any real rest.

Now much of her worry concerned David. She had been making fine progress with the lad and she didn't want the business of the torn painting to ruin everything. Particularly she didn't want David to get the idea she had accused him of doing the damage. She had no idea how his aunt would approach him in the matter and she was anxious to talk to him first if she could manage it. She planned to be downstairs early so this should not be too difficult.

She had no idea how far Elizabeth would go in trying to prove the boy guilty. But she was convinced that this business of attempting to pin the blame on the nine-year-old was merely a diversion.

It did not seem possible she could continue on in the house after all that had happened. And yet she knew that she would despise herself if she fled and left all the questions that were plaguing her unanswered. If only Ernest were back, she would feel she had one sincere ally in the grim old house. She knew she could count on Will Grant as well, but he was not close enough to be of help in a crisis such as she'd encountered tonight.

Originally she had come here chiefly to try to find out who she really was. Now this no longer seemed nearly so important to her. Her concern of the moment was for Ernest Collins. She was filled with a desire to clear his name of the crimes that shadowed him and see him enjoy a measure of happiness.

She was certain the phantom that had threatened her more than once was one of the members of the strange household. And the reason for the attacks might have something to do with Ernest Collins and the mysterious death of Stella.

With these troubled thoughts she fell into an uneasy sleep. She woke several times before morning and was up shortly after dawn. Her body ached; she felt generally miserable. But by the time she had washed and dressed she felt a little more like facing the problems of the day.

It was only a little after seven when she hurried down the stairs to the dining room. She hoped to be able to talk to David there before the others came down. So she entered the big room with anticipation, only to receive a fresh surprise. By the sideboard, helping himself to breakfast, stood Ernest!

His sensitive features glowed with his smile as he put down his plate and came over to take her in his arms. "Surprise!" he said. "My plane arrived in Bangor late and I drove down in the night. I didn't want to be away from you an hour longer than was necessary." He kissed her.

With his lips still on hers, an uneasy thought crossed her mind. Ernest, by his own admission, had spent at least part of the night in the house. How could she be sure he had not arrived earlier than he pretended and been there when the phantom had entered her room and destroyed the painting?

CHAPTER 10

It was so good to have Ernest back again and he seemed so happy that she almost at once dismissed the idea that he had been involved somehow in the night's unhappy episode. She also hesitated to tell him about what had happened, not wanting to mar his homecoming. But after she had listened to his account of the concert tour for several minutes, it occurred to her that Elizabeth or some of the others would arrive before she could tell her version of what had happened, so she quickly interrupted him to inform him of the weird destruction of the painting.

As he listened he grew increasingly troubled and when she finished, he said, "Of course David didn't do it. I can't imagine Elizabeth accusing him of such a thing!"

"She said there had been similar incidents with him to blame."

"It's true he has done some spiteful damage from time to time," Ernest said. "But he'd not be interested in that painting. I doubt if he knew it existed. And why should he destroy it?"

"Why should anyone do such a thing?"

His handsome face had set in grim lines again and she hated herself for bringing this new trouble to him. He said, "I have my own theories about that. I'll tell you later. First, let me talk with Elizabeth."

When Elizabeth came in to breakfast shortly after, he took her aside. Victoria did not wait to hear what was said, but he must have convinced his cousin that she had made an error, for David was not taken to task. In fact, as far as she knew, the boy was not told about the incident at all.

She spent the usual morning session with him and not until it was nearly noon did she see any of the others. It was Elizabeth who appeared in the library shortly after David had left to go out to the garage.

The mistress of Collins House regarded her with annoyance. "I had no idea you were such an accomplished troublemaker, Miss Winters."

Victoria rose from behind the desk. "I don't understand you."

"I think you do. And I'll have you know I don't appreciate your interference or your trying to turn my cousin against me!"

"You're very wrong!" she said, baffled at the venom in her employer's manner.

"Don't tell me you didn't run to Ernest with your pathetic little version of last night's affair," she went on. "I should think you'd have been too ashamed of your hysterical display to mention it. But then, you had to do it to place me in a bad light."

"I said nothing against you!"

"You told Ernest that I was unjustly accusing David of destroying that painting! Do you deny it?"

"I didn't say that. I told him that I didn't think David did it."

"As a result my cousin, with whom I have always been on the best of terms, accused me of being unjust and demanded that I say nothing to the boy."

Victoria gestured despairingly. "Whatever your cousin told you was his thought, not mine."

"After you had cleverly prejudiced him against me," Elizabeth went on. "Now I'll not be able to chastise David and I'll never properly be sure whether he was guilty or not."

"I'm sorry you're so upset about this," Victoria said. "I'm sure when you've had more time to think about it you'll not blame me."

"I've already been doing some thinking," Elizabeth said in her most cutting manner. "And I'm beginning to wonder if perhaps you are the one who damaged that painting."

"That's ridiculous!" Victoria protested.

"You can't deny you were wildly hysterical last night," the older woman reminded her. "I don't think you have any idea what you did."

"If I was hysterical," Victoria said with some defiance, "I had reason to be."

Elizabeth arched her lovely brows. "Of course," she said. "I forgot! Phantoms!" And she went out, leaving Victoria confused and angry.

When she went up to her room she found that the painting had been removed. Either Elizabeth had taken it when she tidied up the place or Ernest had come in and gotten it. In any case she was glad to have it gone, since it served as a reminder of the previous night's horror.

At lunch Ernest came to her and said, "I'll meet you at the cliff after you finished the afternoon lessons." He glanced toward the others who were already seated at the long table and added in a low voice, "It's impossible to discuss anything here."

She nodded her agreement. To her surprise, Elizabeth showed no hint of the animosity she'd displayed earlier. In fact, the older woman went out of her way to be pleasant to her and include her in the general conversation. Victoria was left with the conviction that Elizabeth was not only an accomplished actress but a woman with a will of iron, who would let nothing stand in her way once she had set her mind on a plan of action.

David was restless and failed to concentrate on his studies during the afternoon session. He seemed so listless that she began to wonder if Elizabeth might have been right after all. He was certainly not his usual alert self.

She paused in their geography lesson to ask him, "David, did you see the painting in my room?"

He gave her a wary glance. "The one Stella did?"

"Yes."

"Sure, I saw it lots of times," he replied with boyish arrogance.

"When did you see it last?"

He wrinkled his forehead. "I don't remember."

"Not yesterday or early last night?" she went on. "I don't suppose you went up to my room looking for me last night?"

He shook his head. "No. I was in the garage until it was time for bed. Morgan was working on the truck and I was helping him."

Victoria knew that he had reached the stage where he was interested in cars and liked to pretend he was a mechanic assisting Morgan. She said, "You're certain."

"You can ask Morgan," he said.

That seemed to settle it. David appeared to have an alibi whether it was a valid one or not. She was glad to let the matter drop and resume their work on the geography lesson. At least she could tell Ernest when she met him that she'd questioned the boy and was quite sure he was innocent.

It was a dark day with a touch of fog in the air and so she put on her trench coat before she went out to meet Ernest. He had said he'd be at the cliff and so she headed straight for the footpath that led to it. He was waiting for her as he'd promised. She could see his tall figure as he stood with his hands pushed deep in his topcoat pockets, staring out towards the ocean. When he noticed her approach he came down the path to meet her.

"It seems I've been here for ages," he said. "It's a dreary spot on this kind of a day."

She looked down at the jagged rocks below and the angry foam of the waves that lashed them. "I find it a little awe-inspiring at any time," she admitted. And then she told him about her talk with David.

"Of course he didn't do it," Ernest said.

She gave him a sharp look. "You sound as if you knew who did."

"That's possible, too," he said, looking desperately unhappy.

"Who?"

"Roger."

"No!" she exclaimed. "He wouldn't! What makes you think so?"

"I have good reasons," Ernest told her. "You know how Roger is where women are concerned. Stella wasn't here long until he began bothering her. She put him in his place. And I don't think he ever forgave her."

She eyed the handsome Ernest incredulously. "And you think he'd be mean enough to take out his spite that way?"

"He wouldn't do it when he was sober," Ernest assured her quickly. "But by the time that damage was done last night he'd be well along with his brandy. He may have decided to barge into your room and when he saw the painting went ahead on a drunken impulse and slashed it to bits."

"You're accepting Elizabeth's story that it was done when I was away from the house," she said.

Ernest gave her an odd look. "Driving with Will Grant, I understand."

"He's a friend of yours," she reminded him somewhat awkwardly.

"He used to be a friend of mine," the young violinist corrected her sternly. "He's not anymore. Not after last summer."

"He offered me a drive and it was a nice evening," she said. "I didn't think there was any harm in accepting."

"And when you came home you found your room filled with ghosts," Ernest said with a wry smile. "He must have told you some interesting yarns about us and the house."

She ignored this remark and said, "I did hear strange sounds. They terrified me. I'd heard them before."

He looked away. "Perhaps it's just as well all this has happened," he said. "It has made a few things clear to me. I see now that we were wrong to think there could be any future for us."

His words cut through her like a sharp blade. The strange aloofness that had come over him as he stared grimly out at the fog-shrouded water made her remember Will Grant's warning.

After a moment of silence she said, "You didn't feel that way before you left."

"I was foolishly optimistic," he said, still turned away from her. "The best thing you can do is leave here. Forget we were ever friends."

"That won't be easy," she said quietly, studying him with sad eyes.

"You know what I'm like," he continued in a tone of pathetic weariness. "The mess my life is in."

Again she hesitated. Will had warned her not to press him too far, not to ask for explanations. Yet she felt she must make at least some effort to save the small promise of happiness that had been theirs.

She said, "I believe I'm in love with you, Ernest. Why have you suddenly changed toward me?"

He flinched slightly, but he still stood there motionless on the fog-wreathed cliff, careful to avoid looking directly at her.

When he answered his words came slowly, as if he were choosing them with great care. "There are too many things you don't understand," he told her. "Things I could never hope to explain."

Victoria spoke before she realized the danger to which she might be exposing herself. She said, "You mean about the girl in Santa Barbara and Stella?"

Ernest turned toward her angrily, his eyes blazing. "So Grant did tell you! I guessed that he would."

"It makes no difference, darling," she pleaded softly, reaching out to touch his arm and comfort him.

He thrust her hand away and told her, "If you think it makes no difference, you're either a fool or you're lying to spare my feelings."

The vehemence with which he hurled these words at her told her how deeply he was scarred. Will Grant must be right. Ernest was insane and had been responsible for those terrible things. The young lawyer had warned her that when he was faced with making a decision about marrying her, his love would change to hatred. He was still bound to the dead Elaine.

She searched his tortured face with troubled eyes. "You must have loved Elaine more than any man should love a woman to let her loss do this to you."

He stared at her blankly and in a small flat voice said, "You think you know all about it, don't you?"

"I'm trying to understand!"

"You could never understand!" His voice lifted in anger again.

"Ernest, I want to help you," she pleaded. "No matter how wonderful your yesterday with Elaine may have been, you can't live in it forever. Let me offer you a tomorrow."

"You think you can? That I will ever be able to forget? That I will ever be free?"

"It's up to you!" she insisted. "You must have the will to save yourself. I don't care what they think you've done. If there was any blame, it was because you were ill. Don't let yourself slip back into the dark! There's only one hope! You'll have to put aside this obsession about Elaine!"

'He shook his head slowly. "She'll always haunt me," he said. "She'll always be with me!"

Victoria was near tears. "I can't help you if you don't care! If you're going to sacrifice your life and your sanity to a memory!"

"Don't try to change things!" he said. "You're a wonderful girl. You have a fine future ahead of you. Don't throw it away on me!" He turned and walked swiftly off.

She watched as he followed the path along the cliffs, the path that finally led down to the rocky beach. When his tall figure was lost in the swirling mist, she turned slowly to go back. Her eyes were blurred with tears and her heart filled with an ineffable sadness. Until this meeting she had been certain that his life had reached a changing point, that she would be able to help him in a future they would share.

Now all her hopes were crushed. It was all too easy to believe what Will Grant had told her. Ernest was a psychotic, maybe a dangerous one. In his twisted mind she would gradually take on the image of an enemy. Then he might attack her, as he had the others.

She frowned as a frightening new thought came to her. Perhaps he had been carrying out his double role all along. Perhaps it was Ernest who had terrified her so and who had tried to take her life in the dark cellar room. If he were truly mad, he might not even have any recollection of his actions anymore than he remembered the other crimes.

It saddened her to realize she was quickly swinging around to Will Grant's point of view. She blamed herself for listening so readily to the young lawyer's theories about Ernest. It had biased her and made her alert for any behavior on his part that could confirm what Will had said. Just now he had been so strange he really seemed to be mad. Yet she wanted desperately to hold onto her original conviction that he was innocent, that he was simply an unhappy man caught up in a puzzling sequence of tragic events.

She was halfway back to Collins House when she saw Carolyn waiting for her on the path. She wore a plastic raincoat and a kerchief. As soon as Victoria was near enough to see the other girl's expression, she knew she was aware of her meeting with Ernest.

"I followed you out to talk," Carolyn explained. "Then I saw Ernest waiting and knew you wanted to be alone with him." She stared at her. "You look so unhappy now. You two must have had an argument."

Victoria gave her a wry smile. "It was something more than that. Something more final."

"Don't quarrel with him," Carolyn pleaded. "He needs you."

"I wish he felt the same way," she said forlornly.

"It's Mother!" Carolyn spoke up angrily. "I'm sure she's trying to interfere between you and Ernest. She has always been so possessive toward him. She tries to rule him as she does the rest of us." She glanced back in the direction of Collins House bitterly.

Victoria considered the hostility Elizabeth had shown since Ernest's return and was almost prepared to believe her daughter's statement. Yet she knew, in fairness, the trouble went much deeper than that. Her real antagonist had been dead for years. Her enemy was Elaine!

She told the girl, "It's hopeless to try and come to any understanding with him. He's still in love with Elaine."

"Why do you say that?"

"Because he told me just now. He claimed he would never forget her, never be free of her!"

Carolyn offered her a questioning glance. "I wonder if that means the same thing as saying he loved her?"

It was a good question. Surely a love such as had existed between Ernest and Elaine had an evil, destructive force. The young violinist's present shattered state bore witness to that. She asked Carolyn, "Was she so beautiful?"

The girl nodded. "As I remember her, she was. Of course, I was still a child and didn't see too much of her and Ernest then. They traveled a good deal."

"I've never seen her picture," Victoria said.

"Ernest saw that they were all burned after she died," Carolyn said solemnly. "She was horribly scarred in the accident. It seemed to do something to him. He couldn't bear to look at any of her photos afterward.

Victoria's eyes opened wide. "I don't understand him at all. That sounds more as if he hated her. I'd think he would want to preserve her beauty in her pictures."

Carolyn sighed. "I've wondered about that. Ernest is a very complex person." They resumed the walk back to the house.

"I may decide to leave soon," Victoria said.

Carolyn looked startled and unhappy. "Please don't! Not now!"

"It seems pointless for me to stay after what's happened," she said. "I only regret having to leave David."

"You've been so good for him."

"He's a bright child," she said. "He's almost old enough to be sent to a good boarding school. Or he could surely attend the school in Collinsport."

"Mother doesn't want him in the Collinsport school," Carolyn told her. "And I don't think she'd agree to his being sent to a boarding school."

"It would be better for him than here," Victoria said as they reached the front steps of Collins House. "One day soon she'll have to admit that. Surely his father must see it too."

"Roger doesn't care," the other girl said. "He's a charmer but not much of a parent. He'll go along with whatever mother decides." And they went into the house.

For the benefit of the others, Victoria tried to pretend that nothing had happened. She spent an hour before dinner reading in the library and once again as she left it she met Elizabeth Stoddard coming up from the cellar.

The mistress of Collins House acted slightly more amiable than she had on similar meetings. "You should go to bed early this evening," she told her. "You look wan after your broken rest last night."

"I plan to," she agreed.

"Have you seen Ernest?"

"Not for a while."

"He's been out of the house nearly all afternoon," Elizabeth worried. "I must say he's been in a strange mood since he returned."

"I'm sure he'll be back in time for dinner," Victoria said. "I think he took a stroll to the beach."

Elizabeth frowned. "Not a nice day for it," she said. "But he probably wants to be alone. He's had these spells before. I think what happened to that painting upset him."

"I'm sure that it did."

The older woman sighed. "I suppose it will always be a mystery now. But perhaps it's just as well that it should be." And with this rather surprising statement she went on.

Victoria thought she knew what had been meant. No doubt Elizabeth had now come around to her cousin's opinion that Roger could have done it. Exposing him would only create a nasty situation and there would be no way of reprimanding him. So better to allow the riddle to remain unsolved.

She still found it hard to accept Ernest's new attitude and she was tempted to try talking to him again after dinner. But remembering Will Grant's warning, she decided to allow a little time to pass. Perhaps she might be more able to reason with him later.

Dinner proved a difficult experience. Elizabeth was subdued and spoke little. Carolyn, apparently infected by her mother's manner, said hardly anything as well. Roger was extremely talkative and frequently smiled smugly at Victoria across the table. It was almost as if he knew about her trouble with Ernest and was delighted.

"Allowing the weather to depress you, Victoria?" he asked her over his heaping plate of lobster salad. "You seem in very dull spirits this evening."

"It hasn't been a pleasant day," she said.

"The fog is good for your complexion, my dear," Roger went on in his vein of annoying good humor. "Very often the things we picture as trials turn out to have real benefits for us."

Elizabeth gave her brother an annoyed glance. "I had no idea you were developing into a philosopher, Roger."

He was maddeningly serene. "You live long enough in Maine and you're bound to become one." He fixed his eyes on Ernest, who had just made a belated appearance in the dining room. "Am I correct, Ernest?"

The young violinist gave him a weary glance as he went over to the sideboard to fill his plate. "You generally are," he said. "Or, at least, you're never open to argument."

Roger laughed. "I'm not like the rest of you," he said. "I take life as it comes. You might be wise to follow my example."

Ernest took his place at the table. "I'll consider it," he said without enthusiasm. He gave Victoria a searching look as if to try and gauge her mood.

She pretended a casualness she didn't feel and managed to take some part in the conversation dominated by Roger. She was glad when the meal ended. Ernest vanished upstairs almost as soon as dinner was over. For an hour Victoria sat in the drawing room, reading to David from one of Hawthorne's works. Although he was well able to manage children's books himself, he liked to be read aloud to. From time to time he would halt her to ask the meaning of a term or some information on the novel's historical background. She enjoyed going over the book and experiencing it again through the youngster's inquiring mind.

Soon it was his bedtime and Elizabeth took him to the kitchen for his usual light snack. Victoria lingered in the drawing room talking with Carolyn until darkness had fully settled. Then, feeling utterly weary, she excused herself and started upstairs to her bedroom.

The night light had been turned on in the upper hall and she found herself debating whether she would leave the bed lamp on for the entire night. It would give her a feeling of security, but she felt childish, giving in to her fears this way.

Opening the door of her room, she advanced in the darkness towards the lamp on the bedside table. Then, glowing at her through the shadows, she saw a pale white face floating over her bed. She went rigid with terror, unable to move or shout, staring at the placid, lovely face with horrified eyes. It remained suspended in the blackness—a cold, white face of the dead!

At last she was able to utter a piercing scream. Then she turned and ran from the room. She was leaning against the bannister at the head of the stairs when Elizabeth arrived. She was weeping and incoherent, and could only point to the door of her room. The others gathered swiftly.

She was hardly aware of them or what was happening. After moments of confusion, Elizabeth returned and solicitously put an arm around her. "Someone has played a hateful joke on you. Come, and I'll show you."

Victoria allowed herself to be led back to the room. The bed lamp had been switched on and Elizabeth led her close to the four-poster.

She pointed. "There is your ghost!"

With fear still showing on her attractive face, Victoria glanced up and saw what the older woman had indicated. It was a life-like white mask, hanging by a cord from one of the bed posts. In the darkness it had appeared as a floating head. "Yes," she said in a whisper. "That's what I saw!"

"Damned frightening thing," Roger said, going close to it. "Been painted with some sort of luminous paint."

"You know where it came from, don't you?" Elizabeth said in a cold voice. "And who it is."

Carolyn's face was white and stricken. "It's Elaine, isn't it?" she gasped.

Roger turned, his own face ashen, and nodded. "That's right. It is Elaine. I remember this thing was made by that sculptor friend of theirs. Sort of a death mask. It used to hang in Ernest's study."

"What used to hang in my study?" It was Ernest who spoke. He had only now arrived and was standing in the doorway. Before anyone could reply he saw it himself. A strange expression crossed his handsome face. He came into the room and haltingly advanced toward the four-poster and the hanging white mask.

"How did that get here?" he asked in a tense voice.

"I don't know," Elizabeth said. "It was here when Victoria came in. Someone left it here to frighten her."

But Ernest hardly seemed to have heard her, so intently was he staring at the mask of the lovely Elaine. He spoke like someone in a daze. "I looked for it when I came back. Someone had taken it. I searched for it everywhere."

"Well, at least you've found it," Elizabeth said. "Now the question is, who had it all this time and why did they leave it here?"

Victoria listened to the older woman and had the feeling that she was carefully playing a scene, that none of this had been any surprise to Elizabeth. Elizabeth might have been the one who'd taken the mask from Ernest's house and secreted it away until she'd decided to make use of it.

But before Victoria could pursue this thought any further, she was shocked into attention by Ernest's next act. Savagely he snatched the clay mask from the post and threw it on the carpet. His face pale with fury, he deliberately ground the mask to bits under his heel. Then he turned and strode out of the room.

CHAPTER 11

No one said anything. Within a few minutes the others had left, except Elizabeth, who remained to clean up the mess left by the broken mask.

Victoria knelt to help her and between them it was a small task. Elizabeth took the dustpan with the crushed particles of clay and dumped them in the wastebasket.

Her lovely face was grim as she turned to Victoria. "It was an interesting piece," she said. "Perhaps the last link with Elaine left. It's unfortunate it had to end this way."

"I don't think Ernest realized what he was doing."

The older woman looked bleak. "I wonder," she said. Moving toward the door she added, "I suppose it's useless to suggest you get a good night's rest now, but it is what you need most."

"I'll try," Victoria promised.

Elizabeth paused with the door partly open. "I intend to get to the bottom of this," she said. "No doubt whoever put the mask in here did it while you were in the drawing room reading to David. Be sure and bolt your door."

Victoria promised she would and they exchanged good-nights. Then she was alone in the room again. If she'd had any question in her mind of leaving the bed lamp on before, it was settled now. She knew she couldn't sleep in the darkness after this.

So she had seen the legendary, beautiful Elaine at last. At least, she'd seen the mask. But so great had been her fear and confusion that she could recall little about the calm, white face other than the features had been even.

She would not soon forget the anguish on the young violinist's face when he had come into her room and discovered the mask of the dead Elaine. Nor could she quickly dismiss the picture of him in his almost insane frenzy as he'd destroyed the piece. Surely this proved beyond any doubt that he was mentally ill.

But what bothered her equally was the question of who had put the mask there to terrify her. Not even Elizabeth tried to suggest this was David's doing; she herself had pointed out that he had been in the drawing room with Victoria when it was done. In any case, it was not the sort of thing a child would do. Nor had David any means of getting his hands on the mask; it had been taken from Ernest Collins' own home.

From Victoria's point of view Elizabeth seemed the most likely suspect. Her possessiveness toward Ernest was a strong motive. Victoria was sure Elizabeth did not approve of her close friendship with the violinist. And the woman who had kept herself a prisoner in the great, dark mansion for eighteen years could not be regarded as completely normal. From her furtive manner it seemed she had some secret to conceal.

What the secret might be Victoria could not guess. But she felt strongly it might have something to do with those frequent visits to the cellar. Could it be linked with the husband who had so mysteriously vanished eighteen years earlier? And had any of this a bearing on the puzzle of her own origin?

Victoria was tormented by these thoughts as she prepared for bed. When at last she lay back on the pillow she found her weary body aching for sleep. She closed her eyes with the lamp still burning and hoped that in spite of everything she would gain the hours of rest she needed so badly.

She was almost dropping off when she was alerted by the scraping noise. This time she sat up at once and stared in the direction from which the sounds came. It was the same as on those other nights. The scraping seemed to emanate from behind the oak paneling.

Once again a chilling fear possessed her, but she forced herself to watch and wait, given courage by the lighted lamp. She held her breath as the scraping grew louder. Again she was reminded of long, talon-like nails scraping the surface of the wood. The sounds were more like that than anything else she could imagine.

When she felt she could stand it no longer, a strange sight presented itself to her fascinated eyes. A section of the oak paneling swung silently into the room, revealing an aperture. Standing there framed in it, a flashlight in her hand, was Elizabeth Collins Stoddard!

Victoria was stunned. And the older woman seemed surprised as well. She came out into the room and faced her. "I suppose I have startled you," she said. "I'm a little upset myself. I didn't know the passage ended in this room, although I suspected it."

Victoria got out of bed and threw on her dressing gown. "What passage?" she asked.

Elizabeth glanced back toward the aperture. "I've been puzzled by your stories of hearing strange sounds in this room and also your insistence that someone got in here, in spite of the door being locked and bolted. When I left here tonight I decided I couldn't postpone my investigation another minute, so I found my flashlight and went to the cellar."

"And you found a passage that leads up here?"

"Yes. I remembered a discussion between my mother and father that I'd heard long ago, at the time when they assigned me this room as a child. They said something about the secret stairway and then no more was said. Apparently they decided it would be best not to tell me about it. I was only a youngster and I forgot all about their talk until tonight. Then I began to believe a secret stairway to this room might exist. That is what induced me to make my midnight examination of the cellar area directly beneath this part of the house."

Victoria was still on edge and not positive she could believe the older woman's explanation. This might all be part of a clever scheme on Elizabeth's part to throw her off guard. She said, "So now we know someone did use the passage to enter this room?"

"Yes," Elizabeth agreed. "I'm sorry that I seemed to doubt you. I may as well admit that in the beginning it all seemed preposterous."

"We still don't know who came up here!"

"That shouldn't be too hard to discover," the older woman said grimly. "And now that we know about this secret entrance to your room, there will be no problem protecting you. I'll have Morgan install a padlock on the lower door first thing in the morning and I'll keep the key myself."

"I'll rest easier after it's done," Victoria said.

"One other thing. I don't think we should say anything to the family about this."

"If you think we shouldn't."

"Let us keep it our secret until the guilty one gives himself away," Elizabeth suggested.

"Have you any idea who it might be?"

"Yes. And I think I can promise you there will be no repetition of the unpleasant happenings."

Victoria sighed. "I'd like to believe you."

"You can. But not a word about this to anyone. You understand?"

It was an odd request, she thought. In a way it reinforced her suspicion that Elizabeth was deeply involved in what had happened—or was even the chief instigator. She wished she could talk to Ernest about it.

"Was it hard to find?" she asked.

"Not really," Elizabeth said, "once I had narrowed it down to the section directly beneath here. There's an actual door, but it was concealed in an ell."

"Yet at least one other person must know about it," she said, staring straight at Elizabeth to see if she would reveal any sign of guilt.

The older woman took it coolly. "At least one other person," she agreed. Glancing around the room, she added, "If you like, we can drag a table over and place it in front of the entrance. That will give you some protection."

"I think we should," she said.

They selected the largest of the several tables in the room, and after Elizabeth had swung the concealed door closed, placed the table tightly against it. The mistress of Collins House surveyed their work with satisfaction. "I think that will do," she said.

Victoria asked a question that had been troubling her. "Do you believe Ernest could know about that secret stairway?"

"Why do you mention Ernest?"

"I don't know," she said. "He's been so strange since he returned. I suppose he must be as familiar with this house as any of you."

"That's true," Elizabeth said. "As a youngster he was always over here. We used to play hide and seek in the cellar."

"Perhaps he came up the stairway one day."

Elizabeth looked at her strangely. "So you think it may be Ernest who has frightened you and threatened your life?"

"I don't know what to think," she confessed.

"I'll give you a word of advice," Elizabeth said briskly.

"Don't believe all the dreadful things you may have heard about my cousin. And don't judge him by what took place in this room tonight." Then she moved across to the door. "I must go. Think over what I've told you."

The following day was warm and sunny. Victoria missed Ernest at breakfast, but Roger was there, full of information.

With a roguish smile he told her over his coffee, "If you've an eye out for Ernest, I may as well tell you he's not here. He's gone over to his own place. Said something about leaving here for a while and making arrangements to rent it before he went away."

"Isn't that a rather sudden decision?" she asked as she joined him at the table.

"I'd say so," the blond man said. "But then you can't tell a thing about Ernest. Take the way he behaved last night. Shocking thing for him to smash Elaine's mask. Especially since he's supposed to have gone off his head through grieving her loss."

"People show grief in many different ways."

"So it seems," Roger said dryly.

"I understand he resents anything that reminds him of Elaine's beauty because of the peculiar circumstances of her death." She paused. "I mean her disfigurement in the accident. Surely the sight of that mask must have been a terrible shock to him. Considering that, don't you think his action might be understood?"

"Not by me. But then, I'm not the sensitive type, Victoria." He grinned at her. "And you might be interested to hear we're having this gorgeous day because a hurricane is on its way up the coast. In fact, the weather is supposed to change by night. By tomorrow the full blow will be on."

"I've never been in a coastal town in bad weather," she said.

"Then you may be in for an experience," Roger told her. "Of course, there's a chance the worst of it will head out to sea. But even the tail of a storm can be nasty enough." He rose from the table. "I'm going down to the company docks to see what they're doing about the fishing vessels. You can't keep too close a check on management, you know." He strode off importantly.

Victoria was next approached by Carolyn, who now had her new car. "It's such a grand day," she said. "Let's go to the village and shop. Mother says you can give David the afternoon off from his studies, since there won't be many more days like this."

Victoria hesitated. "I still have plenty to do here."

"Please come along," Carolyn pleaded. "It's no fun going alone."

In the end she gave in. They met at the garage, where surly Matt Morgan was busy at a work bench he'd rigged up at the far end of it. Carolyn's new car was a convertible like the other one, but dark in color. As they drove along the narrow road toward the highway, she chattered about many things.

Quite abruptly she asked Victoria, "Was my mother in your room late last night?"

Knowing that Carolyn might have heard, she said, "Yes. She came by to see that I was all right."

"I heard her," Carolyn said. "Is that all she wanted?"

Victoria frowned and glanced at the girl behind the wheel. She could not read the expression on her face. "We talked for a few minutes," she said. "That was all."

Collinsport was fairly busy. The shabby main street was lined with cars parked at an angle on each side, leaving scant space for moving traffic. The largest of the stores was the Collins General Store.

"It's ours," Carolyn announced parking her car in front of it. "We own this store, the hotel and movie house. They're planning to close it and build a drive-in-theatre."

Victoria smiled. "I see you don't miss any chance for profit."

"Depend on that," the other girl laughed as they got out of the car to enter the store.

"Good afternoon, Miss Stoddard," a suave male voice said from behind them, causing both girls to turn around. Standing with a faint smile on his face was a striking man in a perfectly-tailored gray tweed suit.

"Mr. Devlin!" Carolyn said in a pleased manner. "I wondered if you'd gone away."

"I was in New York for a few days," the man said. He gave his attention to Victoria, staring at her with his piercing eyes. She felt a small thrill at the obvious magnetism of this mystery man of whom she'd heard so many speak. She was so overwhelmed by his sudden appearance that she barely heard Carolyn making the proper introductions.

"Well, Miss Winters," Burke Devlin said, "do you like our little town?"

She nodded. "I find it interesting."

The piercing eyes twinkled. "Interesting, eh? That's a good, safe comment—one I could certainly make myself. And I have the feeling you may find it even more interesting as time passes."

Victoria wondered what he meant by that. Before she could gather her thoughts, he had questioned Carolyn politely about her mother's health and then, with a nod of farewell to her, gone on down the narrow street.

Carolyn touched her arm as they headed for the store again. "Well, you've met Burke Devlin at last! Isn't he a romantic type?"

Victoria managed a small laugh. "That's your reaction to every male!" But she knew the girl was right. Burke Devlin was a man not easily forgotten.

She was unfamiliar with country general stores and so this one fascinated her with its pungent odors and its long counters and many shelves stocked to overflowing with foods, hardware, clothing, leather goods and a sample of just about everything devised by man for sale in a retail outlet. There was a round cheese on display and a big barrel filled with delicious-looking pickles. She was enchanted with the big store and had no trouble filling in her time while Carolyn shopped.

They had been there no more than ten minutes when the door opened and Victoria turned to see Will Grant come in. He joined her at the candy counter where she had been inspecting the various offerings.

"I didn't expect to see you here," he said, smiling.

"And I thought you were in Boston at a convention," she said.

"I was. But nothing much was happening, so I decided to get back here," he told her. "Another reason I came early is that we're scheduled for a bad blow along this coast. I wanted to see that precautions were taken at the plant and the boats were all in ample shelter."

She smiled. "You could have spared yourself the trouble. Roger hurried off this morning to do that very thing."

"Really?" He looked amused. "I had no idea he'd developed such an interest in the business. He's rarely in his office when the golfing is good."

"Give him credit for a fresh beginning."

"I'd like to. But I doubt if it's that. More likely the novelty of knowing the storm is on the way." He glanced across the store where Carolyn was at the hardware counter making some purchases. "Are you shopping as well?"

She shook her head. "No. I came along as ballast." She laughed.

"In that case, why don't we take a stroll down to the docks? I can show you the plant from the outside, at least. It's too nice a day to stay indoors."

She nodded. "I'll tell Carolyn we're leaving," she said, "and ask when she wants to have me meet her at the car."

Carolyn gave her a half hour and waved to Will. Within a few minutes they were standing on one of the wharves looking at the cannery and Will was telling her what each of the various buildings was used for. She was impressed by the scale of the plant's operation.

Finally Will turned to her and said, "Now to get down to some more serious business. What about Ernest? I know he's back."

Victoria's face shadowed. "You turned out to be a kind of prophet."

"Oh?" Will's bronzed face showed interest.

"He's acted just about as you said he would," she went on with a sigh. "I don't understand it at all."

"I've been worrying about you," he said. "If we hadn't met I would've driven over there this evening."

"I've never seen Ernest in such a state. This morning he went across to his own place. He's talking about renting it and leaving Collinsport altogether."

"I wonder why the sudden interest in renting," Will Grant puzzled. "He's let it go empty for years. And he doesn't need the income it would bring, though I admit the place wouldn't deteriorate so quickly if it were occupied."

"It's part of this new mood that's come over him," Victoria said. And she went on to explain all that had happened since she'd seen Will and included a full description of the discovery of the secret stairway and the business of the mask.

The young lawyer frowned. "It looks as if Ernest is as guilty as I've always suspected. Probably Elizabeth is in on it too. I can't believe she suddenly discovered that secret stairway. She must have known about it for some time."

"I feel the same way."

"With all these weird goings-on you're not safe there," he warned.

"I don't think it's any worse than it was," she countered. "I may even be better off than before."

"I can't see that. You've come up against the same quirk in Ernest's mind as that girl on the West Coast and Stella did. And you know what happened to them. Do you plan to remain there until he turns his insane fury on you?"

Victoria gave him a forlorn look. "I know you'll think I'm out of my mind as well," she said, "but I'm still hoping you're wrong. There may be some other answer."

He shrugged hopelessly. "In the face of all you know, what can I say? Do you enjoy being in danger?"

"No. But I want to be certain before I condemn him."

He looked at her hard. "By the time you're certain, you may not be as healthy as you are now."

"It's not as if I'm alone in the house," she protested. "Carolyn has the room next to me. And there is Roger."

"Don't count on him! Don't count on anyone," he said. "Just tell me how long you're going to keep on with this dangerous game."

"I'll wait a few days," she said. "I want to talk with Ernest again."

"Be careful."

"I promise."

"And be especially wary of Elizabeth," he said seriously. "I don't like that secret stairway story at all. I've known her ever since I took over the legal affairs of the cannery, but I can't say that I've ever felt close to her."

"She considers you a good lawyer, but doesn't endorse you beyond that," Victoria told him with a faint smile.

"Well, at least she gave me some credit. There's something more behind that eighteen-year sojourn at Collins House than faithfulness to the memory of a missing husband. It wouldn't surprise me if Ernest and his lovely cousin were two of a kind."

"Now you're indulging in suppositions again."

"Have we anything else to go on?"

"Not much, I admit," she said. "My half-hour is up. I'd best be getting back."

Reluctantly he accompanied her up the wharf and onto the hilly main street. "When will I see you again?" he asked. "You'll be coming out to the house soon, won't you?"

"Probably not until after tomorrow. The next night, perhaps."

"That won't be long."

He was walking with his hand lightly grasping her arm and now he tightened his grip for a moment. "It will seem long to me," he said.

Carolyn was waiting for her in the car. After she'd exchanged a few words with Will Grant, they began the drive back to Collins House. The sun had suddenly gone in and now the sky was gray and threatening. However, it was still unseasonably warm, even with the light breeze that was blowing. She thought that Carolyn had become strangely quiet and preoccupied. The teen-ager usually chattered on even while she was driving.

As they turned off the main road Carolyn said, "You like Will Grant, don't you?"

"He seems very nice," Victoria admitted.

"Do you like him better than Cousin Ernest?"

Victoria gave the girl a startled glance. "That's a strange question."

"I really mean it."

"I don't think I can answer. I haven't really compared them. Ernest can be a wonderful person when he likes."

Carolyn kept her eyes on the road as she nodded. "You mean when he's not like he was last night."

"I suppose I do," she said.

"Perhaps he isn't all to blame," Carolyn continued. "You might feel differently about him if you knew all the story."

"That could be," she admitted. "But I do know pretty much all that has happened. I think I understand him."

"I'm not so sure," the other girl said quietly.

Victoria stared at her. There was no question that there was something distinctly odd in her manner—as if she might be on the verge of offering her some startling revelation.

She said, "If there's anything you know that you think I don't, I wish you'd tell me."

"Maybe I will," the girl behind the wheel said.

But she did not pursue the subject. She started talking about the store and its endless variety of goods. The abrupt switch exasperated Victoria, but she went along with it, hoping Carolyn would decide to tell her whatever it was she had planned too. But if Carolyn didn't bring up the question of Ernest again, Victoria intended to face her with it.

They parked the car in the garage and she helped Carolyn gather up the various parcels to take into the house. There was no one in sight, not even Matt Morgan. And the old mansion seemed especially ominous under the dull gray skies. The sticky heat was another weird touch to an afternoon of strange weather.

Carolyn glanced around the yard as they walked to the rear door. "Neither Roger nor Ernest is back yet," she said. "I don't see their cars."

"They'll likely arrive in time for dinner," Victoria said.

The house was deathly silent. Victoria guessed that David would be out somewhere, but she had no idea where Elizabeth might have gone. She thought of the cellar. She seemed to spend an increasing amount of her time down there.

"I'll look for Mother," Carolyn said. "I'll see you later upstairs."

Victoria left her and went up to wash and change for dinner. She decided she would wear something summery, since it was so hot, and found a green linen that she thought would be suitable. A glance at the table barring the hidden entrance to her room showed her it had not been moved. She found this reassuring.

She studied herself in the mirror and was satisfied. The green dress made her dark hair more striking. She thought of her meeting with Will Grant and what the young lawyer had said. In many ways he was right. But she intended to stay on at Collins House at least a few more days. There was always a chance that things would work out, that Ernest would return to his real self. There was always a chance, but now it seemed very slim to her.

The room suddenly seemed miserably warm and uncomfortable. She went over to the casement windows and flung them open, but the warm air that rushed in was the opposite of the tangy, salt-water breeze she was used to. The silence, the dark skies and the unusual humidity combined to give her a depressed, uneasy feeling. And so, when a gentle knock came on her door, she turned around with a start. Realizing her reaction had been overwrought and a trifle ridiculous, she went to see who it was.

Opening the door, she saw that it was Carolyn who had changed to a thin white dress. The teen-ager beckoned her to join her in the corridor. "Come with me," she said. "I have something to show you." It was only then that she noticed the key ring with a half-dozen heavy keys in the girl's hand.

Making a joke of it, she said, "You look like the keeper of the dungeon."

"Or something," Carolyn said. And she led Victoria into another corridor that ran at right angles to the main section of the house. It was a corridor that she had never entered before and she guessed it connected with one of the deserted wings.

Carolyn at once confirmed her guess. "I'm taking you out to the rear section," she said. "This is where Ernest had his apartment up until last year."

"I've heard you speak about it," Victoria said as they came to the end of the damp-smelling corridor and Carolyn carefully selected a key to unlock the door.

The key turned easily and the door opened to reveal a small, neatly furnished living room. Carolyn went in first and then turned to her with a covert glance. "You mustn't ever tell Mother I brought you up here. She'd be furious."

Victoria's eyes opened wide. "But why?"

"She wouldn't want you coming in here," the other girl said. "She doesn't want anyone to know."

Again she was startled at the girl's mysterious behavior. She looked around the room. "How many more rooms are there to the apartment?"

"Five rooms altogether," Carolyn said. "They open one off

the other." And she led her through the series of rooms, musty now from being closed up for a year. At last they came to the small kitchen and stood facing each other.

Victoria was mystified at the whole business. She couldn't conceive why Carolyn wanted to show her the deserted apartment. She said, "I can't understand why Ernest asked to live here in this isolated section of the house and why he needed so much space. A room in the main house, such as he has now, is much more sensible. I can't see why he'd want a place like this to live in alone."

Carolyn's eyes were over-bright as very quietly she told her, "But when Ernest lived here, he wasn't living alone."

CHAPTER 12

There was a long silence. Victoria suddenly felt faint, as if her mind refused to function. The heavy musty smell and the dark shadows of the small kitchen seemed to close in on her. Then she forced herself to struggle out of the abyss of nausea and unreasonable fear.

"He wasn't living alone here?"

"That's right," Carolyn said. "You mustn't ever breathe a word of this. I don't know what Mother would say if she knew I was telling you. She and I are the only ones who know. But I want to tell you so you'll understand about Ernest.

"Go on," she said weakly.

"It happened before Uncle Roger and David came, so they don't know either," Carolyn said. She hesitated, nervously licking her lips as if unable to find the right words. "When Ernest lived in this apartment, Elaine was here with him."

"Elaine!"

Carolyn's young face was solemn. "Yes."

"But that's impossible! Elaine's been dead for years."

The other girl shook her head. "She didn't die in that accident, Victoria. She recovered. But she was so badly disfigured— mentally, too—that Ernest spread the word she had died and then took her to that house he bought in Santa Barbara."

Victoria stared at her with incredulous eyes. "It's too fantastic!"

"And yet it's true! All of it! He did it for her sake, because he couldn't bear to see her as she was, I suppose. He planned to live in retirement and care for her. But he didn't realize how dangerously insane she had become. When he became friendly with that girl, Elaine waylaid her in the garden one night— they lived nearby. She beat her across the face with a chain and almost killed her. The police suspected that Ernest had done it. He barely escaped serious trouble. He knew that he couldn't cope with her alone any longer, so he came back here."

"No!" Victoria shook her head. "You must be making this up!"

"Believe me, I'm not. He had written Mother before and asked her to help and let him have an apartment in this section of the house. Of course she agreed. She didn't want to see him get into any more trouble and she hoped Elaine would be happier here and perhaps make a partial recovery. They came in the night. Ernest hurried her into the house and up to the apartment. I only saw her veiled head." She gave a small shudder. "She would never allow anyone to see her face."

"And she and Ernest lived here for a year?"

"Yes. She got no better and she gave him a dreadful time. Mother, as well. I never came near this part of the house and I tried to forget she was here. But there were times when she had those spells and her screams could even, be heard downstairs. And then once in awhile she would play her violin. You'd know how it would end. She'd break off without ever finishing the piece. There would be the sound of wild discords and then silence."

"Couldn't anything be done for her?"

"Ernest tried. They might have helped repair her face if she hadn't been in such a bad mental state. He waited, thinking she might improve. And then Stella came to live in the cottage. She and Ernest became friends. He should have known better than to allow himself even the innocent sort of relationship they had. The crisis came when Stella fell or was pushed over the cliff. He could never be certain whether Elaine had followed the girl on that foggy night and was responsible for her death or if it had been an accident. But he did know that Elaine had escaped from the house that night. He found her wandering out by the cliff after midnight."

"How awful!" Victoria said.

"That finished it," Carolyn said with a sigh. "As soon as the fuss died down about Stella, he told Mother he was going away on a tour and asked her to have Elaine committed to a private mental hospital while he was away. He couldn't bring himself to do it."

"And she's still alive and in a mental hospital now?"

"Yes."

"So that's why he's acted so strangely," Victoria said.

"I felt you had to be told," Carolyn said. "It wasn't fair that you should go on not knowing."

"Is she in a hospital near here?"

"No. In Boston," Carolyn said. "I don't know the name of it or any of the details. I don't want to. It's all too ugly and horrible."

"I agree," Victoria said in a low voice.

"I was in Bangor for a two-week holiday when they came for her," she said. "I've never questioned Mother about how she behaved when she knew she was being taken away. But when I returned I could tell it had been an ordeal. Mother's been nervous ever since."

"Not much wonder."

"We'd better go back," Carolyn said quickly. "I don't want Mother to miss us. And you will promise me faithfully not to let her know I told you."

"I promise," she said, not really thinking of what she said. Her head was reeling with the misery of her thoughts. She followed Carolyn silently out of the musty apartment and waited while she locked the door again. When they returned to the main corridor Carolyn gave her a furtive farewell and hurried downstairs, presumably to return the keys to their usual place.

It was time to join the others for dinner, yet Victoria felt she could not sit down at the table and pretend that nothing had happened. Carolyn's revelation had changed the whole picture for her. If the girl's story was true, and she had no reason to doubt that it wasn't, it exploded all Will Grant's theories about Ernest's being an insane killer.

Elaine had been the guilty one. Elaine, who was supposed to be dead and who had actually been living in Collins House such a short time ago. It was Elaine whom Ernest had been shielding. And for her he had lived under the shadow of suspicion. No wonder his nerves had given under the strain.

And no doubt this was why Elizabeth had behaved so oddly lately. She, too, had shared the burden of the mad Elaine. It wasn't enough that she had her own tragedy and carried almost the full weight of managing the business; she had been forced to come to the aid of Ernest. It had even fallen to her to supervise the most painful episode of all, the transferring of Elaine to a mental hospital.

This would change all her own plans. She saw the people in the grim old mansion in a different light and she found it difficult to decide how she would adapt to the new situation. One thing was certain. She wanted to speak briefly to Ernest at the soonest possible moment and let him know that she had heard the truth and understood his plight. It would solve none of their problems, but at least it would let him know she still had faith in him.

With Elaine alive, it was unlikely anything would ever come of their brief romance. That much was clear to her. Ernest loved his wife, or at least the memory of the person she had once been, far too deeply to consider marrying again while she languished in a mental hospital. Knowing how he felt about Elaine, Victoria could hardly expect him to divorce her, even though the law would allow it.

She understood now why he was planning to leave. There were far too many unhappy memories for him in the area and this, together with his frustration at not being able to tell her the truth or to continue their romance, had caused him to decide to go somewhere else.

It was nearly six. He should be back by now. She would go downstairs to intercept him before he entered the dining room. She made her way to the foyer and glanced into the drawing room and then the dining room, but he had not put in an appearance. Thinking he might not have arrived yet, she went out on the steps to see if his car was parked in its usual place.

He drove in to the yard at that exact moment. She hurried down the steps and across the lawn to meet him.

He looked gaunt and new lines of weariness were etched on his handsome face. He saw her when she was part way across the yard and she thought for a moment he would turn and get into the car again. But he came to meet her, his expression pained.

She spoke first. "Ernest, I want to talk to you. Before you go inside."

He shook his head. "There's nothing to be said."

"I think there is," she said calmly. "You see, I know about the apartment and about Elaine as well."

Ernest stared at her in consternation. "Who told you?"

"That isn't important just now. Some things I have to say to you are." She took him by the arm and led him across the lawn a short distance from the house where the hedges gave them a degree of privacy. Quickly she told him what she had heard and how she felt about it. She ended with, "I know how you feel, that we can never marry. But it doesn't change my love for you."

The sky had grown unusually dark and there was an eerie stillness in the air that warned of oncoming rain. He stood staring at her in the weird false twilight.

Very softly he said, "Victoria, you're a remarkable young woman."

"Why do you say that?"

"Because you're capable of this incredible sacrifice for me," he told her.

"It hardly compares to the sacrifice you've made for Elaine," she reminded him. "And beside your love for her, mine must seem a puny thing."

His eyes narrowed and he reached out and gripped her by the arms. "My love for Elaine!" he said. "You don't know anything about my love for her! Or why I hate her now! Have hated her all these long years!"

"Hated her!" she gasped.

"It was love in the beginning," he went on quickly. "Until she made a joke of our marriage. She wasn't content with betraying me with one man; she kept on at the game until our love was soiled, shoddy! She was spending a weekend with that sculptor, the one who made that mask, when the car overturned and burned. If there had been any justice, she would have died that night. But she lived on."

"And you proved your love was sincere by protecting her," Victoria said softly.

With a deep sigh he released her arms. "I felt it was my duty," he said. "There was no one else to stand by her. But there was no more love between us. We have existed on a mutual hatred!"

"Poor Ernest!" she said.

"Stella may have died because of Elaine. That is why I had Elizabeth commit her." He paused and studied her with unhappy eyes. "That is why I want you to forget me. I don't want you dragged into a miserable situation that could go on for years."

"Why not let me decide what I want to do?" she asked softly. As she spoke, the first heavy drops of rain began to fall.

Ernest took her arm. "We'll not argue about it," he said. As if on impulse, he drew her to him for a long kiss. When he finally released her, he looked away quickly and said, "We must go inside. The others will wonder what happened to us."

She went with him and as they mounted the front steps, her hand in his, she felt a new peacefulness. It was true that formidable barriers still stood between them and the chance of a happy life together. But she knew their love was strong and true and somehow they would endure and find a way to share the future.

When they entered the dining room the others were all gathered at the table. Elizabeth regarded them with suspicious eyes. "I have been wondering where you two were," she said. "I saw you cross the lawn together."

Victoria spoke up for them both. "It's such a strange evening. We were studying the sky and the ocean until it began to rain."

"I see," Elizabeth said dryly. "Well, I hope your dinner isn't ruined."

Roger said, "There's apt to be more than a few drops before morning. The weather bureau says driving rain and hurricane winds."

She thought there was less tension around the table than there had been for some time, although she sensed a certain coldness in Elizabeth's manner. Several times Carolyn had managed to give her a quick, knowing smile when her mother's attention was engaged. Victoria had nodded to the girl and thought she understood.

By the time dinner was over, the rain was coming down heavily and it was completely dark. Elizabeth hurried off to close any windows that might still be open, while most of the others gathered in the drawing room. Carolyn switched on the lights in the two crystal chandeliers that had first served the old house with candles, then lamps and finally had been wired for electricity.

As Ernest and Roger talked together by the window, Carolyn managed to take Victoria aside and in a low voice ask, "How did you make out with Ernest?"

"Fairly well. We didn't have long."

"I knew you must have told him," the other girl said. "Somehow you both looked so much happier when you came in."

"We are. Thanks to you." Victoria smiled at the teenager.

Carolyn returned the smile. "Too bad it's such an awful night or we could all go in and celebrate at the Blue Whale."

"I don't think we have that much to celebrate," Victoria said. "And I'm sure your mother wouldn't approve of the Blue Whale again."

"She approves of Joe Haskell and he spends most of his time there."

Victoria laughed. "That's another story."

Elizabeth returned and they sat talking for a while as the storm continued to grow worse. None of them seemed to want to be alone in their rooms before it was time to go to bed. The rain lashed against the large windows at the front of the house and the howling wind had a frightening force. It was just before ten when the lights in the big chandeliers faded.

Roger stood up staring at the subdued glow from the ornate fixtures. "It looks as if we're going to lose the lights," he said.

David, who had been sitting on the floor by his father, smiled. "Gee! This is going to be fun!" he exclaimed.

Elizabeth gave him a reproving glance. "Not when you have to go up to bed with a candle."

The lights came up briefly and seemed normal again. Victoria let her eyes wander along the paneled walnut walls of the great room and her gaze had just fastened on the grim portrait of the founder of the dynasty, Isaac Collins, when the lights faded sharply again and this time went out.

"That's done it!" Roger exclaimed. "Get the candles, Elizabeth."

Within a few minutes candles had been found and placed in various spots to light the room. And now it was time for them to go upstairs. Ernest escorted Carolyn and Victoria to their respective doors. He looked romantically handsome with the candle highlighting his face. After Carolyn had said goodnight and gone into her room, he lingered for a moment with Victoria.

"Candles seem to suit this grim old house," he smiled. "Don't you agree?"

"They fit in very nicely," she said. "And it's lucky, since we're not liable to have any other light tonight."

"Perhaps for several nights," Ernest told her. "When a bad storm like this hits the coast the lines go down everywhere. It takes a while to get them all repaired. And we're a long stretch from the main road."

"Somehow the storm doesn't bother me," she said, smiling in the glow of her own candle. "Perhaps it's because I feel differently."

He shook his head. "I can't stop you if you want to believe the impossible," he said.

"Sometimes that's the only way to make it come true," she reminded him.

He placed a hand on her arm and his eyes showed a new tenderness. "I told you earlier you were a remarkable young woman," he said. "Now I'll say it again." And he bent forward to kiss her briefly.

She went into the darkness of her own room, filled with more hope than she'd known in a long while. Placing the candle on her bedside table, she smiled faintly. It might take time, but she no longer had any doubt that things would work out.

By the time she was in bed the storm seemed to have reached a new peak. The shutters that creaked and groaned in a regular wind now strained and clattered in the wild gale. She could almost feel the house give with the storm and the casement windows rattled and threatened to burst open each time a new gust of wind and rain hit them.

She tried to sleep, but between the storm and her racing thoughts she had no success. Her mind kept going back to the apartment and the unhappy Elaine living there. She shuddered at the thought of what that mutilated face must look like and at the cunning madness of the damaged brain. It was incredible that Ernest had managed to cope with her so long. Probably he couldn't have done so without Elizabeth's help.

Now Elaine was in an institution where she would be under proper restraint and receive treatment. She made up her mind to ask Ernest more about the hospital in the morning. It was important that he keep in touch with the doctors and find out about his wife's condition and if there were any hopeful signs.

The wind lashed at the casement window again and she glanced quickly to see that it was still shut. Then she heard a knock on her door, soft at first, but repeated a little louder. Thinking it must be Elizabeth or Carolyn, she quickly got up and put on her dressing gown and slippers and hurried across to open the door.

When she did, the corridor seemed to be empty. Straining to see if there was anyone there in the darkness, she advanced a step or two outside. She was unable to see anything and decided she must have imagined the knocking. Or perhaps Carolyn had become frightened standing alone in the corridor and had gone back to her room. She decided to try the other girl's door. As she moved forward she heard a rustle behind her and suddenly felt the touch of an unseen hand on her arm.

A soft feminine voice whispered, "Don't try to get away! I have a knife. It's pressed against your back and I won't hesitate to use it."

Victoria was close to fainting. She asked, "Who are you?"

"You'll know soon enough," the voice said. "Keep your voice down and go toward the stairs. Try to break away and I'll kill you! I'm more used to the dark than you are!"

The surprisingly strong hand urged her forward and up the short flight of stairs to the upper floor. Victoria was still unable to see and the howling wind and rain were creating such a pandemonium she doubted that she would be heard if she risked a scream. And if her captor's threat meant anything, a scream would surely bring cold steel driving through her flesh.

She tried to guess the identity of the phantom creature who guided her along the upper corridor and could only think of Elizabeth. Elizabeth, who had so often aroused her suspicions. Elizabeth, who had brought her to this strange house in the first place.

"Stop!" the phantom voice whispered.

Victoria did as she was told and then was aware of a door being opened and a sweep of rushing wind and dampness suddenly hitting her face.

"Up the stairs again," the voice commanded.

"Where are you taking me?" she asked.

There was a chuckle. "You've been up here before." The cruel hand shoved her forward.

Victoria stumbled and then groped her way up the narrow steps. As the sound of the storm increased in fury and she felt the impact of wind and rain she knew she was being herded up the narrow steps to the captain's walk on the roof of Collins House. It would be the most exposed spot in this violent storm. Only a lunatic would think of going up there.

She halted half-way up and said, "I'm going no further."

"Would you rather die here?"

She turned, trying to make out the figure so close behind her, but could not even see her outline. She said, "You're bluffing!"

Her answer was immediate. There was a quick movement and then a sharp pain in her arm. She let out a cry of anguish, "No!"

"I could just as easily have driven it into your back," the voice said, and the venom in it chilled her.

Her arm was burning from the wound. "Who are you?" she gasped. "Why are you doing this?"

"You should know. You're trying to steal my husband."

New horror filled her. "Elaine!"

There came a soft chuckle. "The others tried it and I settled with them. Now it's your turn!"

Victoria huddled against the wall of the narrow stairway. "I don't believe you! You're lying! You can't be Elaine! She's in a hospital!"

"That's what you and he thought." The tone was thin and cruel. "But Elizabeth lied. I played on her sympathy. She didn't send me away. She hid me in the cellar. That's where I've been ever since."

"The cellar!" Victoria repeated in a whisper, remembering all Elizabeth's furtive excursions down there. It all fitted. The creature behind her must be Elaine.

"Oh, I've managed to find my way up into the house when I wanted to. I saw you and him on the cliffs that day. And I saw you this afternoon. But you'll never be together again!"

"Then you—" Victoria whispered, "you're the one who came into my room. You slashed the picture. You left the mask."

"Yes," Elaine said coldly. "I did all that. I wanted you to leave this house. But you wouldn't go. And when you had that accident with the car—it was an accident, you know—I thought Fate would help me. But nothing frightened you, did it? Well, that's too bad, Victoria. It's too bad you were so brave, because now you are going to die for it."

"We can't go any further!" Victoria protested. "Let me free and I promise to help you. Ernest and I will do all we can for you!"

The harsh chuckle in answer to this had no sanity in it. "Go on," Elaine said, prodding her with the knife. "On to the roof."

Victoria thought quickly. She knew she was dealing with a madwoman, a madwoman who might possess incredible strength and who also was holding a weapon which she did not hesitate to use. To attempt a struggle on the cramped stairs would give her adversary all the advantage and almost surely mean her death. Her best hope was to obey Elaine's instructions and brave the storm-ridden captain's walk. Step by step she moved slowly upward, playing for time and trying to plan her strategy as she went. Elaine pressed close behind her and finally they emerged out into the driving wind and rain.

She turned to see the veiled figure come toward her and knew that Elaine's plan was to send her plunging over the railing down that great drop to the gravel driveway below. She would be found there in the morning, another unexplained suicide. She dodged quickly, but Elaine came after her, the knife still unraised.

Victoria struggled to grasp the hand with the weapon and keep it away from her, at the same time battling fiercely to prevent being forced closer to the railing. Elaine fought with the strength of the insane and twice she had her bent far back over the low iron rail. It would only take just a little more to send her hurtling down through the stormy darkness.

The rain soaked them and the surface beneath their feet was wet and slippery. Victoria hurled the madwoman back and found herself free for a moment. But it was only for a moment. The dark, veiled figure came forward again with a shrill scream and one of the claw-like hands reached out to her, gouging at her eye and ripping down her cheek. Victoria was beginning to weaken. She felt she could not keep up the battle much longer. With the desperation of a final effort she grasped the madwoman by the shoulders and tried to swing her against the railing. As she did so Elaine slipped and lost her footing. With a hoarse cry of fear she toppled back over the low iron rail. Victoria was almost taken with her. For a moment she leaned weakly against the rail, staring down into the dark where her opponent had vanished, minding neither the wind nor the rain.

"Victoria!" she heard her name called from the stairway and knew it was Ernest. She staggered forward to meet him and then slumped in a faint.

It was not until much later that she heard the full story of how Ernest had carried her down to her bedroom and Elizabeth had taken care of her until the doctor could be summoned from the village the following morning.

It was Elizabeth who had alerted Ernest after going to the cellar room where she'd been keeping Elaine and finding her gone. She had confessed the deception quickly and warned him of the possible danger to Victoria. A hurried journey to her room had disclosed her absence and after that it was merely a matter of following them to the roof.

The storm passed as quickly as it had come. Two days later a quiet funeral service was held for Elaine in the small stone church in Collinsport. She was buried in the family lot in the ancient cemetery adjoining the church. Victoria was not well enough to attend the service with the others, but Ernest told her about it when he visited her in her room later that day.

She could see that the day had brought many memories back to him. It was no time to voice thanks for his new freedom. That could come later. Now the tragedy of Elaine and all those wasted, unhappy years was much too close.

His handsome face was grave as he sat at her bedside. "I've been thinking," he said. "I believe it will be best if I stay with my original plan and leave Collinsport for some time. I'll rent my place and take an apartment in New York. I can travel out on my tours from there."

She was sitting propped up against several pillows and she studied him with a new tenderness in her eyes. "That sounds like a good idea," she agreed.

"I want to give you some time," he said. "And myself, as well. Perhaps in six months or a year we can think about more definite plans."

"Yes," she said in a soft tone little more than a whisper.

"This house should hold no more fear for you," he said. "Elizabeth wants you to stay on with David. I hope that will be your decision."

"I'll stay," she said. "I still have to try to find out some answers about myself. I think my best chance is here."

"Just to be sure you won't forget me," Ernest said, "I'll promise I'll write you at least once a week."

"And I'll answer," she said.

He gave a deep sigh of relief. "I knew you'd understand," he said. And he leaned forward and took her in his arms for a long and tender kiss.

And in that moment of sheer happiness she knew that it had all been worthwhile. One day she and Ernest would come together again and perhaps there would be no more partings. In the meantime she would go on as governess to David. She would live on here in this quaint village and try to pry further into the secret of her past. She could not easily forget her meeting with the mysterious Burke Devlin and wondered if he might be able to help her. The Collins family had come to seem like her own—perhaps one day she would discover this to be true. In any event, she looked forward to the weeks and months ahead. She could cope with Roger; Carolyn was lovable, and she could get to know the gracious Elizabeth Collins Stoddard better in the strange old mansion by the sea, Collins House!

AVAILABLE NOW FROM HERMES PRESS

Book Two: *Victoria Winters*
Book Three: *Strangers at Collins House*
Book Four: *The Mystery of Collinwood*
Book Five: *The Curse of Collinwood*
Book Six: *Barnabas Collins*
Book Seven: *The Secret of Barnabas Collins*
Book Eight: *The Demon of Barnabas Collins*
Book Nine: *The Foe of Barnabas Collins*
Book Ten: *The Phantom and Barnabas Collins*
Book Eleven: *Barnabas Collins vs. The Warlock*
Book Twelve: *The Peril of Barnabas Collins*
Book Thirteen: *Barnabas Collins and the Mysterious Ghost*
Book Fourteen: *Barnabas Collins and Quentin's Demon*
Book Fifteen: *Barnabas Collins and the Gypsy Witch*
Book Sixteen: *Barnabas, Quentin and The Mummy's Curse*

...and over a dozen more thrilling *Dark Shadows* editions!

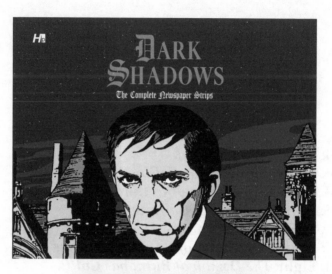
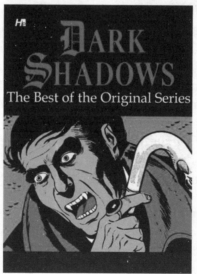